Frozen in Time

Murder at the Bottom of the World

Book I in The Antarctic Murders Trilogy

Theodore Jerome Cohen

AuthorHouse™
1663 Liberty Drive
Bloomington, IN 47403
www.authorhouse.com
Phone: 1-800-839-8640

©2010 Theodore Jerome Cohen. All rights reserved.

No part of this book may be reproduced, stored in a retrieval system, or transmitted by any means without the written permission of the author.

First published by AuthorHouse: 8/5/2010

Without limiting the rights under the copyright reserved above, no part of this book may be reproduced, stored in or introduced into a retrieval system, or transmitted in any form or by any means—electronic, mechanical, photocopying, recording, or otherwise—without written permission from the author. The scanning, uploading, and distribution of this book via the Internet or any other means without permission is punishable by law. Your support of the author's rights is appreciated.

ISBN: 978-1-4520-0272-9 (e)
ISBN: 978-1-4520-0270-5 (sc)
ISBN: 978-1-4520-0271-2 (hc)

Library of Congress Control Number: 2010904080

Printed in the United States of America

This book is printed on acid-free paper.

Cover Design by Chandra Rose, AuthorHouse
Book Design by Katie Schneider, AuthorHouse

Back cover photograph of author by Martin Halpern, PhD, Base Bernardo O'Higgins, Antarctica, January, 1962

Because of the dynamic nature of the Internet, any Web addresses or links contained in this book may have changed since publication and may no longer be valid. The views expressed in this work are solely those of the author and do not necessarily reflect the views of the publisher, and the publisher hereby disclaims any responsibility for them.

To my beloved Susan

■

"Great God! This is an awful place!"

Captain Robert F. Scott
British Royal Navy Officer and Explorer

Upon reaching the South Pole in 1912

■

Contents

Preface

This is a work of fiction based on real events that took place between 1958 and 1965. It depicts many actual events and people in my life, though some situations and all of the dialogue are pure invention.

Real names are used in cases of people who have passed away. The names of living persons (with the exception of my family member's first names) have been changed. For my family, the name "Stone" has been substituted for "Cohen" to acknowledge the fact that considerable license has been taken in telling the tale. Some characters are totally fictitious, as are the names of some agencies and organizations, both military and academic.

Theodore Jerome Cohen
Langhorne, PA

Acknowledgments

Virginia Smith, EdD, reviewed and edited early versions of the manuscript. I am extremely appreciative of her many suggestions on how I could improve the storyline as well as the development of certain characters. Michael Garrett's careful editing resolved several problems related to style. The Rev. Msgr. Michael J. Carroll, Director, Office for Ecumenical and Interreligious Affairs, Archdiocese of Philadelphia, gave generously of his time to answer questions pertaining to the Roman Catholic Church and its sacraments. Maria Luisa Perez provided expert corrections to my faulty Spanish; her contributions were invaluable. The support of Edwin (Eddy) Vile, Jr. and Robin Kemmerer is gratefully acknowledged.

Chilean Antarctic Bases – 1961-2

North Antarctic Peninsula

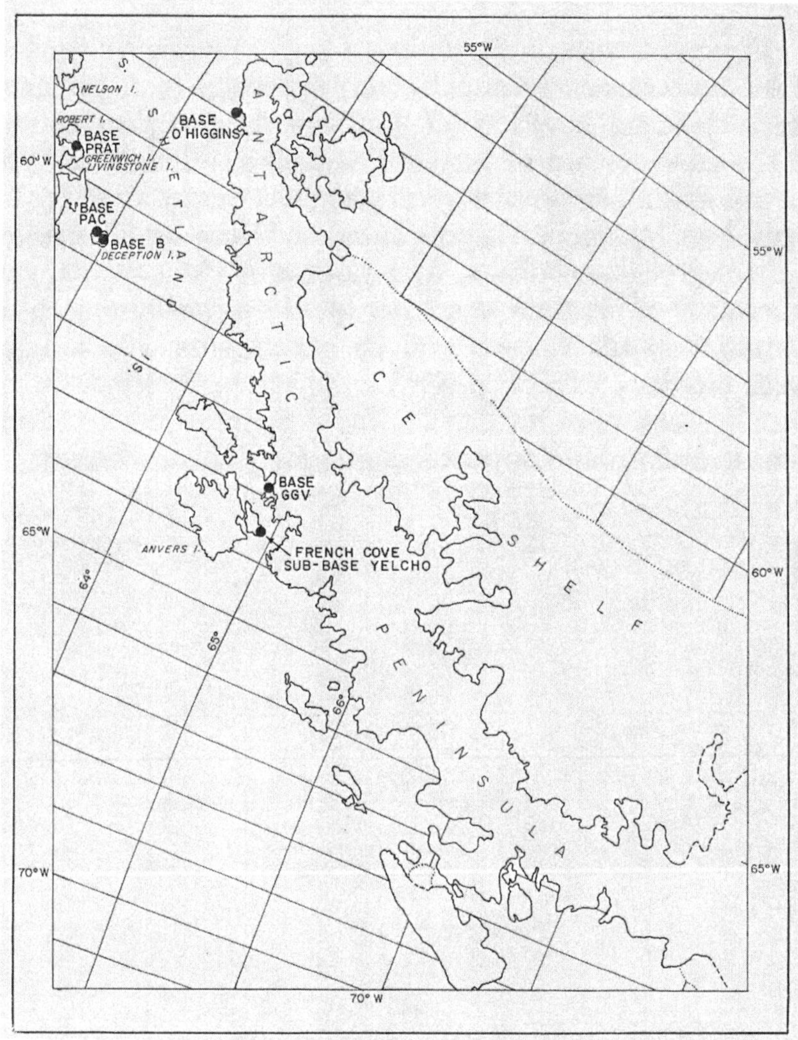

Reference: Theodore J. Cohen, "Gravity Survey of Chilean Antarctic Bases," *Journal of Geophysical Research,* The American Geophysical Union, Volume 68, Number 1, January 1, Washington, D.C., 1963 (From the author's original manuscript, 1962)

Deception Island, South Shetland Islands – 1829

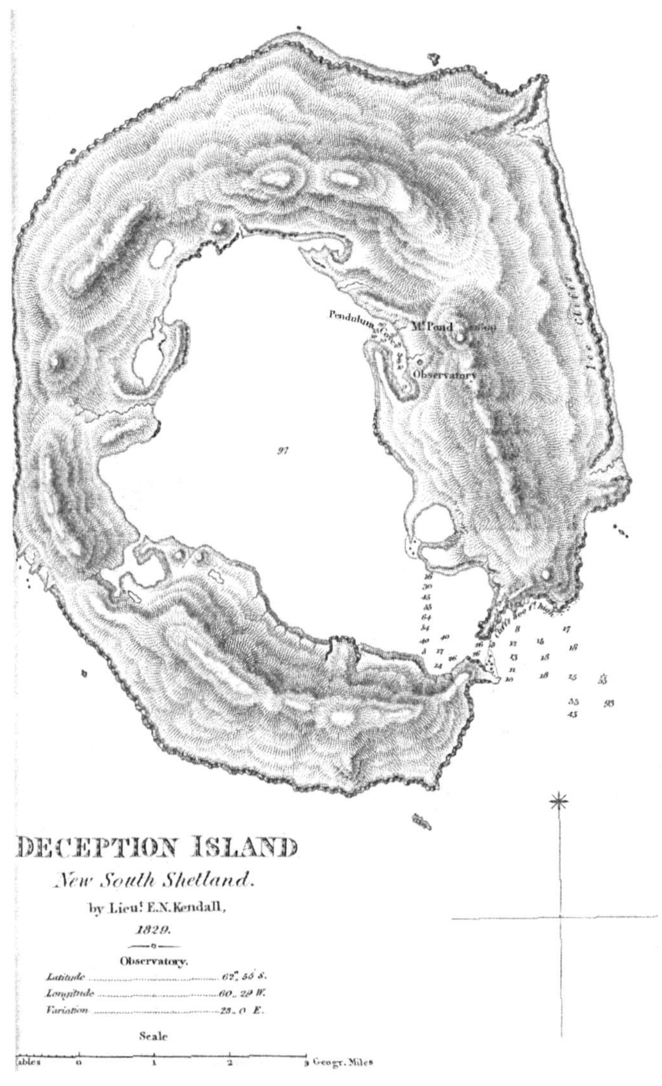

Map Created by Lieut. E.N. Kendall on the First Scientific Expedition to Deception Island, His Majesty's Sloop *Chanticleer*, under the Command of Captain Henry Foster, January 9 through March 8, 1829

(http://commons.wikimedia.org/wiki/File:Deception-Island-Map.jpg)

(See, also, http://www.antarctica.ac.uk/documents/bas_bulletins/bulletin32_04.pdf)

I
Return to the Highlands

Susan instinctively stomped her foot into the car's floorboard, put her hands up in front of her face, and yelled at her husband, "Watch out! You're going to hit him!"

Ted Stone, off in his own world, steered hard-left, narrowly missing the man pedaling his racing cycle toward them on the right side of the roadway. "Dammit! Why wasn't he going with traffic . . . on the other side of the road?" Ted pounded the steering wheel with his right hand and cursed again under his breath, berating himself for almost causing what could have been a fatal accident.

As they continued up the road, Ted reflexibly reached down and rubbed the ugly six-inch scar on his left leg. Even the passage of more than four decades had not erased the outward signs of the tragedy that befell him that fateful day in February, 1962 while he was working on the North Antarctic Peninsula.

The trees on either side of the road had grown significantly during the intervening years. Certainly the brush and hedges had been through countless cycles of death and replanting. But by squinting in the late afternoon sun, Ted was able to project back to a time when, as a graduate student, he made the trip daily from his apartment on Madison's Lake Monona to The Highlands west of the city.

The trip was easier this afternoon than it had been in those days. Then, his 1959 Saab 93F, with its 3-cylinder, 2-cycle engine, the type that required a quart of oil to be added to the gas tank at every fill-up, labored up South Highlands Avenue, its exhaust pipe spewing smoke and emitting the distinct putt-putt sound of a lawn mower. Today, their large rental car slid effortlessly past the back entrance of Brittingham House, former headquarters for the University's Geophysical and Polar Research Center and now home to the president of the University.[1]

In his college days, the dilapidated carriage house at the bottom of the hill behind the mansion was occupied by one of Professor Robert Meyer's graduate students and his family. On weekends, the student's old black Volvo, always in need of a valve job, could be found parked in front of the garage with its hood up, the student's legs projecting from the engine compartment while his ever-present black Labrador lay watching from the dirt under a century-old oak.

Not this Saturday. The carriage house was in pristine condition while the grounds were impeccably groomed, the lush, blue-green grass close-cut by the University's maintenance staff. The trees were trimmed as well. Ted was not sure when the Center vacated the mansion and moved to the main campus in Madison. No matter. The estate, an elegant Georgian-style house built in 1916, had been restored to its former glory and currently was used for official and charitable community events hosted by the president.

---

1 http://helpdesk.wisc.edu/vip/page.php?id=10310

The scene was one of total order and serenity, a place where life for him had once moved forward in increments of time measured by weeks that merged into months, and finally, into semesters that cumulated in the award of degrees. It was a place where he had taken life for granted, with the knowledge that tomorrow would be much like today, which, in turn, would be a lot like yesterday. Worries that there might be no 'tomorrow' never entered his mind, until that trip to the bottom of the world. *At the least,* he thought, *no one* here *is dependent on someone else for survival.*

"It's hard to believe that more than forty years have passed since we last were up here, isn't it?" Susan asked rhetorically, brushing stray hairs from her forehead and taking a sip from a small bottle of water.

Yes, thought Ted, only half-hearing what she had said. His mind still was thousands of miles away, in Antarctica, where he almost had lost his life decades earlier and where troubling questions surrounding events of the distant past still haunted him on many a sleepless night. "Huh? What did you say?"

"I said, it's hard to believe that more than forty years have passed!"

"I'm sorry. I was just thinking about the people we knew then . . . the people I worked with at the Center . . . the people I traveled with to Antarctica. Where are they now? What happened to them? And what *really* happened that austral[2] summer on the Ice?"

Some of his colleagues, unfortunately, had died, including the man who was his first major professor, Professor George Woollard, *the* Professor George Woollard—world-renowned

[2] Southern, or Southern Hemisphere

expert in gravimetry and determinations of the geoid.[3] When Professor Woollard heard that Ted was heading to Antarctica to help a graduate student in the Department of Geology collect rock and fossil samples for that student's doctoral thesis, he insisted—the professor maintained that he used 'gentle persuasion'—Ted take a gravimeter with him. Because there were few gravity measurements at the end of the North Antarctic Peninsula,[4] [5] a new gravity network needed to be established there. The data were needed to assist the University in developing an accurate representation of the Earth's gravity field.

The trip to The Highlands this afternoon was simply for purposes of seeing how the area had changed and of rekindling old memories, a mere side trip following a visit with some of Susan's former classmates who still lived in Middleton. Now, having seen Brittingham House and with their curiosity satisfied, Ted and Susan drove back to Madison's Edgewater Hotel, saying little. His mind still was almost totally focused on the autumn of 1961 and the months leading up to his departure for the Frozen Continent.

The Brittingham Estate brought back a torrent of memories of the four University of Wisconsin scientists who traveled to one of the most desolate regions on Earth. Memories of the two graduate students in geology, Grant Morris, a Canadian, and David Green, who was born and raised in Iowa; their

---

3 The geoid is that equipotential surface that would coincide exactly with the mean ocean surface of the Earth, if the oceans were in equilibrium, at rest, and extended through the continents (such as with very narrow canals). See, for example, http://en.wikipedia.org/wiki/Geoid

4 http://en.wikipedia.org/wiki/Antarctic_Peninsula

5 http://en.wikipedia.org/wiki/File:Ant-pen_map.png

major professor, Ethan O'Mhaille, PhD, a recognized expert in clastic sedimentology[6] and earth history; and Ted, himself a graduate student in geophysics, and of the tightrope they walked between life and death decades earlier.

Morris had been Ted's laboratory instructor in Geology 1b in the spring semester of 1960. This was a year after Ted transferred from the School of Engineering to the School of Letters and Science in his junior year. Ted's need to take additional science courses for purposes of satisfying the School of Letters and Science's requirements for graduation, which led him first to freshman meteorology, then to freshman geology.

Ted, at six feet, was taller than the other students in the geology class; he was also twenty-one years old, three years older than most of his classmates. An extravert who was endlessly interested in others and what they did, he sought out and made friends easily. Before long, he and Morris, who was only a year older than Ted, struck up a close friendship.[7]

Morris, of medium build, was quite handsome, and his female students flirted with him constantly. Always well dressed in slacks, a shirt with a button-down collar, tie, and cardigan sweater, he had a ready smile and answered questions in a straightforward and professional manner. He was the very model of a teaching assistant at a Big Ten University.

---

6 Clastic sedimentology is the branch of geology that studies sediment and sedimentary rocks that are made up of particles that are the solid products of weathering at or near the Earth's surface. See: http://spartan.ac.brocku.ca/~rcheel/teaching/sedimentology/SedNotes/Chap1.pdf

7 While Morris was only one year older than Stone, he was two years ahead of him in school. The reason for was that when Morris entered the Canadian school system, no kindergarten was available. Hence, he entered the first grade when he was five years old.

There was no question as to his scientific prowess. Morris already had made one trip to Antarctica, mapping an area near the tip of the North Antarctic Peninsula and gathering rock samples for his thesis. Single, he spent considerable time in his laboratory working on the development of his thesis or at his apartment studying. However, he also was known to enjoy a good night on the town with his girlfriend, Vivian, a UW senior.

Geology 1b proved to be no challenge for Ted. He easily mastered the material, leaving time during class for him and Morris to discuss Morris's PhD dissertation, or more to the point, Morris's field work in Antarctica. One day, early in May, 1960, Grant approached Ted.

"Hey, Ted, I'm returning to Antarctica in December, 1961," Morris began, "and I'll need an assistant. Are you interested?"

Was he interested? "Hell, yes!

"The timing is perfect, Grant. I'll be completing my Bachelor's degree this summer and starting my Master's degree in September. I should finish by August and be ready to join you!"

"Sounds good to me," said Professor O'Mhaille, when apprised of their plan. And so, Morris, together with Green and Professor O'Mhaille, continued to make preparations through the National Science Foundation (NSF) and the Government of Chile for the University of Wisconsin–Madison team to join the 16th Chilean Expedition to the Antarctic. Meanwhile, Ted worked on completing his Bachelor's degree, and then, continued on with his Master's. Once that was completed, he formally declared his major in Geophysics and joined the University's Geophysical and Polar Research Center to begin preparations for the trip south.

II
The Great Chilean Earthquake of 1960

It was early afternoon, Sunday, May 22, 1960, a sunny, warm day in Madison, with a high in the mid-70s Fahrenheit and light westerly winds. Six thousand miles to the south, all hell was about to break loose.

At precisely 2:11 PM Chilean time, an earthquake measuring 9.5 on the Richter scale, the largest earthquake recorded since seismographic monitoring began, struck Valdivia, Chile. A swarm of foreshocks the previous day, some as large as magnitude 8.0, gave warning of impending disaster, but there was no way of predicting when or where the mainshock would strike or how much energy it would release. The Great Chilean Earthquake, or Valdivia Earthquake, as it is called, was related to fault ruptures from Talcahuano to Peninsula de Taitao, Chile.

Talcahuano, in Chile's Central Zone, is home to the country's main naval base. Thus, when President Cristian Alessandri declared a National Emergency, the full capabilities of the Chilean Navy stationed there were ordered to assist the civilian population of the city. One ship that charged toward Talcahuano was the auxiliary fleet tug *Lientur*[8] under the command of Captain Roberto Muñoz.

One ship that charged toward Talcahuano was the auxiliary fleet tug *Lientur*.[9]

Muñoz, a tall, athletic-looking man with steel-gray eyes and a serious demeanor, was in his mid-30s. A bachelor, he was an honor graduate of the Chilean Naval Academy and an experienced ship's captain. Though born into poverty—his father's employer, owner of one of the country's largest copper mines, sponsored him for admission to the Naval Academy—he was considered by many to be destined for flag command. Muñoz had been passed over once for lieutenant-commander. Some say a ranking member of the Promotion Board, an elitist, liked neither his background nor the manner in which he gained entrance to the Academy. However, the unexplained early retirement of that Board member, a vice admiral, several

8 http://www.navsource.org/archives/09/38/38177.htm

9 Photograph reproduced with the permission of Patricio Villalobos, Captain (Ret.), Chilean Navy, and Gary P. Priolo, NavSource Naval History

months after Muñoz's appearance before the Board, cleared the way for his promotion to lieutenant-commander and subsequent promotion to corvette captain.

Well-respected by all who knew him, the captain gave 200 percent of himself to his mission, his ship, and his crew, which explains much about his life, including his broken nose. "Oh, that?" he would say, matter-of-factly, without cracking a smile. "I collided with the opposing side's goalie on the Academy's *fútbol* field. It was an unfortunate accident that sent *him* to the hospital with three broken ribs and a collapsed lung. When you near the goal line, *mi amigo*, nothing must stand in your way. *Nothing!*"

Muñoz, some said, was a born leader. He spoke with authority and commanded not only for reasons based on his rank and position, but also on his ability to motivate his crew and to convince them of their ability to achieve uncommon results, even when faced with the most difficult of challenges. Above all, his 'force of character' gave him the ability to ask his men to follow him into situations fraught with risk . . . situations that could, in the extreme, threaten their very lives as well as the safety of the *Lientur* itself.

Among the *Lientur's* complement of five officers and forty enlisted men were two non-commissioned officers, Chief Warrant Officer (CWO) Raul Lucero and Chief Petty Officer (CPO) Eduardo Bellolio. They had signed on for three-year tours of duty in late 1959 and were scheduled to participate with their vessel in the 16th Expedition to the Antarctic. Though both were slightly over five feet tall, Lucero was by far the heavier—stout, actually—weighing some twenty pounds more than Bellolio. Lucero had a full head of black hair and massive, muscular arms developed over years of working in naval construction. Aside from one drooping eyelid, the result of a childhood accident, he was a fine physical condition for a man in his late thirties.

Lucero had risen rapidly within the enlisted ranks. Though a chief warrant officer, his record was *not* without blemishes. In mid-1954, the Navy's Office of Internal Affairs found evidence of him apparently having facilitated the transfer of naval supplies to the Chilean black market. Lucero bragged, "The Navy couldn't hang a thing on me."

He was correct. The trail left behind by whomever was responsible was so complex and convoluted that investigators never were able to determine exactly *what* was taken from at least two Fleet Warehouses, much less *the final destinations* of the items stolen. There were indications that a naval officer as well as people outside the Navy may have been involved. However, the evidence was so 'thin' that naval investigators came away empty-handed.

In the end, no action was taken against Lucero or anyone else. After four years of monitoring the suspects' activities, Internal Affairs dropped the matter.

Bellolio was slightly built and a year younger than Lucero. He tended to be hot-tempered and impulsive, thinking little about the consequences of his actions. Though physically agile, he bore a two-inch scar across his left cheek, a constant reminder that others were just as quick as he was with *una navaja de muelle.*[10]

While Bellolio might not admit it, it was Lucero who often kept him out of trouble. "Come on, Eduardo," Lucero would say, "at least keep your brass polished and your shoes shined so you

---

10 Switchblade knife

don't get no demerits during inspection." Without Lucero's help, Bellolio, though proficient at performing his assigned tasks, would most certainly have spent more time than he already did peeling potatoes in the galley.

Both men were covered with tattoos, products of the many parlors found in every port they visited. To them, the artful mementos that adorned their bodies were signs of *machismo,*[11] something to be shared proudly with their brothers-in-arms. The works of art on their bodies depicted their loves, hates, triumphs, and love of country.[12] Lucero was particularly proud of one faded black tattoo glorifying Death that could be found high on his upper left arm.

Neither man had been married, though each had girlfriends in many ports. "I can't wait to return to Punta Arenas," said Lucero. He and Bellolio were making small talk while standing on the stern of the *Lientur* as it steamed at full speed from the waters off Chile's Easter Island toward Talcahuano. "I want to pay a visit to Lucy's![13] You know, Eduardo, you can always have a good time there as long as you are careful about how much money you take with you and how much you drank."

Bellolio was thinking about Lucy's as well. "I'll go back to Lucy's, Raul, you can be sure of that, but it won't be to dance." He was picturing in his mind's eye the young brunette in the red gown who had gotten him drunk during his last visit to that house of prostitution, the one who took two month's pay

---

11 Manliness, virility

12 http://www.tattooarchive.com/history/sailor_tattoos.htm

13 Lucy's, at that time, was one of the most famous houses of prostitution in Chile. There was not a sailor in the Chilean Navy who did not know about Lucy's. Houses such as Lucy's were for more than just prostitution; they also provided men with opportunities to drink and dance with the women who lived there.

from his wallet after he passed out on her bed. *I have a score to settle,* he thought, all the while fingering the folded switchblade knife in his pocket. *She's lucky I didn't discover the money was missing until we were at sea, or she'd already be dead!*

The typewriter was Lucero's and Bellolio's *military* weapon of choice. Each wielded this instrument based on more than two decades of experience manipulating 'the system' to their advantage. Give either of them a typewriter and within a short period of time, the movement of men and supplies throughout the Chilean Navy could be accomplished with a few lightning-fast keystrokes. Lucero, however, had elevated his mastery of manipulating the Navy's transportation and warehousing system to an art.

Each man entered the Navy at the same time, immediately after finishing their secondary school education. However, Bellolio's rank was two levels beneath that of Lucero's. This was the result of a Navy Board of Inquiry that found Bellolio complicit in the knifing death of an enlisted man some two years earlier during a fight at a brothel in Valparaiso. Bellolio never would talk about it—"I was set up," he maintained—but according to Lucero, the issue involved him making gross, lewd comments to a Yugoslavian prostitute who was dancing with another sailor.

More than thirteen Navy enlisted men and seven prostitutes were involved in the mêlée before the Shore Patrol broke it up. Because of the confusion surrounding the event, the Board was unable to separate fact from fiction. So, while he could have received a dishonorable discharge, the only actions the Board took against him were to reduce his rank, and with that, his pay.

No one aboard the *Lientur* paid much attention to the broad 3-foot-high swell that passed beneath the ship as it steamed toward Talcahuano. It was the tsunami generated by the earthquake spreading across the Pacific Ocean. Soon it would wreak havoc on land masses as far away as Japan and Australia.[14] In some locations, it produced waves reaching heights of eighty-two feet. The tsunami devastated the Hawaiian Islands as well as coastal areas of Japan. More people died as a result of the tsunami than of the earthquake. Before it was over, total fatalities resulting from the earthquake and tsunami were estimated at 6,000.[15] [16]

Upon reaching the Port of Talcahuano, Captain Muñoz was forced to anchor offshore while the docks were repaired. An aide summoned Lucero and Bellolio to his quarters.

"Lucero, Bellolio," he barked, "take a launch to the pier, and from there, go to the Fleet Motor Pool and commandeer a small truck. Here are your orders. They give you all the authority you need." He thrust the orders into Lucero's hands.

"Then, go down to the Maintenance Shop and take what you need to secure the local office and vault of the Banco Central de Chile. The bank building has been heavily damaged. Restore order around the building. Looters are in the area. You are authorized to shoot them on-sight, no questions asked.

"Report back to the ship by radio at 0900 and 2100 hours[17] daily."

---

14 http://www.drgeorgepc.com/Tsunami1960.html

15 http://en.wikipedia.org/wiki/1960_Valdivia_earthquake

16 http://earthquake.usgs.gov/earthquakes/world/events/1960_05_22_articles.php

17 9:00 AM and 9:00 PM local time

Lucero and Bellolio saluted, executed an about-face, and left. They hastily changed their clothes, gathered personal items and rations, and checked out two M1 Garand rifles and two 45mm pistols as well as ammunition. Within thirty minutes they were on their way by motor launch to the dock. Once there, by presenting their orders, they obtained a small truck and the equipment needed to secure the bank's perimeter. Before leaving the Maintenance Shop, Lucero selected a small gasoline generator, several heavy demolition tools, including a jackhammer and air compressor, which he and Bellolio hitched to the back of the truck, an oxyacetylene torch, and several other cutting tools. "You never know what we're going to find," he yelled to the shop foreman as he and Bellolio wheeled oxygen and acetylene tanks to the truck.

"What do we need all that stuff for?" asked Bellolio. "All the captain wanted us to do was secure the area. I thought this was going to be a nice cushy job, maybe one that would allow us to secure the perimeter, then, take a few shots at some rats."

"You'll have plenty of time to relax when you retire, Eduardo," responded Lucero with distain, "assuming you can ever *afford* to retire. Did you ever stop to think about that?"

Their orders were to prevent all but the highest government officials from entering the bank, but those officials were too busy elsewhere even to visit the site. Thus, Lucero and Bellolio were free to work their way unobserved into the secure areas of the building, some of which had been heavily damaged. There was no electricity. It did not matter. The alarm system was so heavily damaged that even if power were available, the system would not have functioned.

Using their heavy demolition tools and working late into the night, the two men managed to enter the area where the safe deposit boxes were maintained.

"Give me a hand with this table, Eduardo. Now, help me with that desk over there, and we'll put it on top of the table. We need to make a scaffold, or we'll never be able to reach the boxes near the ceiling."

With the makeshift scaffolding in place, Lucero looked up, looked at Bellolio, thought for a moment, and finally came to the obvious conclusion. "You're lighter than me. Grab a hammer and chisel, and climb up there. Break the doors off some of those boxes near the ceiling. Once you get the doors off, pull the drawers out and throw them on the floor. We'll sort through things later.

"And Eduardo . . . don't open all the boxes. Leave some alone, here and there. We need to make it look like the damage was caused by the earthquake. We'll leave plenty of stuff, cash and all, lying on the floor when we're done so no suspicions are aroused when we turn the bank over to the *Carabineros*[18] after they arrive."

Lucero was unrelenting. He drove Bellolio and himself to the limit. Using brute force, the pair succeeded in opening more than 100 boxes over a period of two hours.

Their 'take' was beyond anything they could have imagined. There was an extraordinary amount of cash for the taking, perhaps $4 million in U.S. and £1 million in English currency.

---

[18] Chilean state police. See, for example, http://en.wikipedia.org/wiki/Carabineros_de_Chile

The real prize, however, was the millions of dollars in negotiable securities, gold coins, and jewelry. Among the coins were British Sovereigns by the hundreds: Victoria's, Edward VII's, and George V's; French 20 franc coins: Napoleon III's, Angles, and Roosters; and German 20 mark Wilhelm II's.[19] They also found Brazilian 20,000 reis gold coins; Uruguayan Centenario 5 peso pieces; and $10 Eagle Liberty, $20 Double Eagle, and $20 St. Gaudens from the United States.[20]

"Without counting things up, Eduardo," said Lucero, raising his eyebrows, "I'd say what we have here is worth at least $12 million U.S. dollars!"

"So? What are we supposed to do with it?" Bellolio called down to him. "These coins weigh a ton! The jewelry has to be fenced, and we'll only get a fraction of what it's worth. We can't spend the money right away without someone noticing. And even if we figure out a way to pack everything up, how are we going to get it out of here?"

Lucero did not hear a word he said. He was totally preoccupied with something he had taken from the safe deposit box at his feet.

"Look at this!" he whispered excitedly, though no one could possibly have heard him, even if he had shouted. Bellolio jumped to the floor, took off his gloves, and looked over Lucero's shoulder.

There in Lucero's hands lay open an exquisitely carved, mahogany presentation box. In it, on a bed of pure white silk, was a necklace. Not just *any* necklace, but a spray of sculpted diamond flowers and leaves, accented by collet-set diamond

---

19 http://www.aboutgoldcoins.info/european-coins.html
20 http://www.aboutgoldcoins.info/american-coins.html

and emerald buds on a circular-cut emerald neck chain, with everything mounted in platinum and gold. Tucked inside a silk fold was a folded certificate of authenticity. It had been signed and dated in 1932 from Hammer Galleries of New York City, duly attesting to the provenance of the piece and showing it dating from to the late 1880s. Lucero studied the yellowed certificate, which was torn at the creases. "Look, Eduardo, this here necklace has been in the family for generations. It's a family heirloom. I have a friend up north who will pay a sweet price for this trinket!"

Lucero put his hand into the same safe deposit box and pulled out a small velvet pouch tied with a black drawstring. Opening it, he gently withdrew a man's 1954 Patek Philippe 18K yellow-gold *Genève*[21] wrist watch, easily valued at more than $50,000. Without even knowing who owned the watch, both men knew instantly that he must be a very wealthy person, indeed—perhaps a person of high political standing.

"Wow! Let me see that!" cried Bellolio, grabbing for the watch.

"Keep your dirty mitts off," yelled Lucero, slapping Bellolio's right wrist so hard that it turned bright red.

Bellolio jerked his hand back, rubbing his wrist with his other hand. "Why did you do that for?"

"This is mine! Keep your dirty paws off!" Lucero held the timepiece out in front of him at a distance, there better to savor

---

[21] Made from 1951 to 1956. The basic characteristics include rectangular chronograph buttons and crown partially recessed. There are other features, such as a tachometer scale, applied raised Arabic hours and feuille hands. At least 14 like this are known. The watch is valued today at more than $225,000. See: http://95.110.194.207/CatalogoMasterNewYork/catalogo/MasterNewYork/pdf/high/eng/LOT%2092.pdf

its beauty. "It'll look real nice on my wrist while I'm sipping *caipirinhas*[22] on the beach at Ipanema."[23]

Inflation being what it was in Chile[24]—the value of the currency halved every three years—few in the country's upper class kept their wealth in local currency and investments. Instead, they preferred the safety of U.S. and British currency as well as other defensive alternatives. No wonder these safe deposit boxes held a king's ransom.

Chances were good, too, that the thefts, once discovered, would *not* be reported to the authorities in their entirety, if at all, in most cases. Such reports, after all, could precipitate full-scale investigations of the parties involved and of their secret financial holdings.

Any reasonable thief might simply take *some* of the money, coins, and jewelry, tuck them into his pockets, and continue about his business as if nothing had happened. Not Lucero.

"I think I know how we can get most of this stuff out of here, Eduardo."

Bellolio was all ears.

Lucero was born and raised in Arica, a port city in the north of Chile, just eleven miles south of the Peruvian border. "When I was young, I attended Catholic school at the Catedral de San Marcos with my good friend, Chilean Army First Sergeant Leonardo Rodríguez. In fact, we was altar boys together at the cathedral. He still lives in Arica with his wife, Juanita, and their three children. Every once in a while, I hear from

---

22 http://en.wikipedia.org/wiki/Caipirinha
23 http://en.wikipedia.org/wiki/Ipanema
24 During the 1950s and 1960s, inflation averaged 31 percent per annum. See, for example, http://countrystudies.us/chile/58.htm

him . . . where he's working, what he's doing, how the family's doing . . . that sort of thing.

"Well, Rodríguez is scheduled to rotate into Base O'Higgins with the 16th Expedition to the Antarctic a year from this December," continued Lucero. "Under military regulations, he can take one or two large appliances with him that have been brought into the country from the United States or Europe for sale in Chile—you know, luxury appliances like refrigerators and stoves. And . . ." He paused to heighten the drama of the moment. "And he can store them at the base during the summer."

Bellolio looked at him, tipped his head to one side, and squinted. He looked totally puzzled by what Lucero was saying to him.

Lucero continued. "In March of the following year, when the Expedition returns to Chile, his appliances get shipped back to Arica *without* him having to pay import duties on the original purchase. Best of all, the shipping charges, from the dock in Talcahuano to Antarctica, back to Chile, and finally to Arica, will be paid by the Army. It's a perk, Eduardo—*un incentivo*. It's something offered by the government so military personnel will volunteer for hazardous duty in Antarctica."

"And—?" asked Bellolio, who still had a quizzical look on his face.

"Come on, Eduardo!" yelled Lucero impatiently. "What the hell's the matter with you? Don't you understand nothin'?

"All we have to do is buy a large refrigerator or stove from an appliance store in town, load it with this stuff, repack and reseal the appliance in its original crate—reinforced, for sure—and present it, together with the necessary paperwork, to the

Navy Dock Master in Talcahuano. From there, the crate goes to the Fleet Warehouse here before it gets shipped to Punta Arenas for the voyage to Antarctica.

"Once the Expedition is over and the crated appliance is delivered to Rodríguez's home in Arica, we meet there, uncrate it, take our shares, slip across the Peruvian border, and go our merry ways." Lucero grinned and threw his hands in the air as if the entire matter were a *fait accompli.*

Bellolio was awestruck! He stood there staring at Lucero, his mouth and eyes wide open, acknowledging the beauty and simplicity of the idea. A smile slowly enveloped his entire face. Then, just as slowly, the smile turned to a frown.

"What if Rodríguez won't go along with your plan?"

"You leave that to me. He's always complaining that he never has enough money to provide good things for his wife and family. So, I'll make the refrigerator a gift to him. In addition, I'll offer him cold, hard cash . . . $1 million dollars, U.S. currency.

"Actually, he won't have a choice. By the time he finds out what we did, the refrigerator might already be in Antarctica. Who knows?

"Sometimes you just gotta make decisions for people, Eduardo!"

With Bellolio left to stand guard at the bank in the event Captain Muñoz paid a surprise visit, Lucero set about finding a suitable appliance in which to store the spoils. It did not take long. Business was at a standstill in the city. Merchants were anxious to deal. Prices were exceptionally good.

In no time he returned with a new refrigerator and the necessary sales documents. The unit was a new, imported, top-of-the-line, 1960 Hotpoint 18-cubic-foot yellow refrigerator.[25] He could not stop grinning. “I’m sure Mrs. Rodríguez will love it.”

It took four hours to fill the refrigerator, which all the while remained in its opened crate on the truck’s bed. With foresight borne of necessity, Lucero had made one trip back to the Fleet Warehouse to gather additional blankets and packing material, as well as reinforcing pine strips and strapping before setting out to purchase the refrigerator. This ensured that nothing would impede their efforts to empty the bank’s vault of the cash, securities, gold, and jewelry they wanted to take with them.

“I’ll let Rodríguez know of *our* little plan sometime in the next few months,” Lucero yelled to Bellolio as he drove off to deliver the crate to the dock. “There’s still plenty of time before he leaves on the Expedition. In the meantime, what he doesn’t know won’t hurt him.”

---

25 http://books.google.com/books?id=3kOsUZgXbjMC&pg=PA127&lpg=PA127&dq=refrigerator+1960+Hotpoint+space+age+18&source=bl&ots=mxCnGXJNoA&sig=rC7bKlaOOD5xjKJcMXLa55YnhPU&hl=en&ei=M4BPS8n_CMSa8AbLoO2SCg&sa=X&oi=book_result&ct=result&resnum=3&ved=0CAwQ6AEwAg#v=onepage&q=&f=false

III
Preparations . . . And Second Thoughts

'E-l-e-a-n-o-r? Eleanor! Where in tarnation are those pendulum[26] data from Mexico City? I need to see them before we begin preparation of that paper for the *Journal of Geophysical Research.*"

Could that be Professor Woollard? thought Ted as he stepped through the front door of the Department of Geology and Geophysics' Annex on University Avenue in mid-September, 1961.

The young secretary near the door looked up from her old Underwood typewriter and asked if she could help him.

"I have a meeting with Dr. Wollard," said Ted.

Hearing the name 'Woollard,' the secretary rolled her eyes, threw her left hand over her shoulder, and with her thumb pointing backwards, mumbled something out of the corner of her mouth to the effect that "he's back there . . . you can't miss him."

Professor Woollard was a legend within the scientific and academic communities. He was known worldwide for

---

26 The local gravitational acceleration of the Earth can be calculated from the period of a pendulum. See, for example, http://en.wikipedia.org/wiki/Pendulum#Gravity_measurement

his contributions to geophysics in general and gravimetry in particular, not to mention his lack of patience! Now, Ted was meeting him for the first time.

There he was, a gentleman in his early sixties with long white hair, not quite up to Albert Einstein's standards in length or craziness, but still, long overdue for a cut. He was hunched behind his weather-beaten desk in a small corner office not more than ten feet square, an office covered from floor to ceiling with bookshelves that overflowed with, and sagged under the weight of, a ton of scientific and scholarly journals, periodicals, and publications from all over the world.

A dirty ashtray held two pipes. It sat atop a stack of reprints, each, no doubt, endorsed with the obligatory 'With the compliments of the author' scribbled in the upper-right-hand corner. The balled-up copy of the previous day's edition of Madison's *The Capital Times* in the wastepaper basket probably had not been read; if it had served any purpose at all, it was as the depository for the ashtray's overflow.

As Ted held up his hand to knock on the doorframe, someone brushed past him and walked through the open door. "Give me a moment, honey, will you?" It was the professor's assistant, Eleanor. A middle-aged woman with a pencil in her upswept beehive hairdo, she carried a stack of computer printouts one-half-inch thick tucked neatly under her left arm. Eyeglasses hung from a decorative chain around her neck. She was sweating in the heat of the late-summer weather that had settled over Madison. "If he doesn't see these data now, we won't hear the end of it!"

When the professor was satisfied that Eleanor had applied the proper temperature-correction factors to the data she had just processed, she left the room, giving Ted a wink on her way out.

Woollard turned his attention to Ted.

"You must be Stone," he observed evenly, peering over his bifocals. "Grab a chair from next door and drag it in here."

The two men quickly settled down for a chat. It did not take the professor long to convince Ted of the importance of the International Gravity Network and of the need to acquire additional data at the end of the North Antarctic Peninsula. "The better our model of the Earth's gravitational field," Woollard explained, "the better will be the entire World Geodetic System, the standard used in cartography, geodesy, and navigation."[27] Ted knew something about the force of gravity[28] from his studies in physics. *Even Einstein could not develop a unified theory that included gravity,* he chuckled to himself. *Nature simply will not bend to Man!*

Still, Ted was uncertain as to whether or not he would be able to devote the time and attention needed to do both jobs, the one he would be doing for Grant Morris and the one Professor Woollard now was proposing. But after listening to his repeated requests, Ted finally agreed to assist the professor by establishing a new gravity network among the Chilean Antarctic bases and by linking this network to the International Gravity Network.

"All right, professor, I'll do it."

---

27 http://en.wikipedia.org/wiki/World_Geodetic_System

28 There are four basic forces in Nature: The Strong Force, The Electromagnetic Force, The Weak Force, and The Gravitational Force. See, for example, http://sciencepark.etacude.com/particle/forces.php

"Good!" exclaimed Woollard. He slowly lifted himself out of his chair, shuffled to a back corner, and grabbed a cylindrical shipping container. "This contains Worden gravimeter #14.[29] [30] The manual's in the case. Read it!" He handed the container to Ted.

"Keep this instrument with you at all times, Stone! It cost the University $3000! [31] Eat, sleep, and travel with it by your side until you return it to me in March! If you fly, buy a seat for the damn thing. Don't you *ever* let it out of your sight unless you can trust the person you give it to! And that person better be someone who works for the Department or the Center!"

"Yes, sir!" *I might as well be married to it!* Ted thought.

"There is something you should know before I leave, professor," said Ted.

"And what might that be, Stone?

"There will be times when I'll have to pass the gravimeter to David Green, one of Professor O'Mhaille's graduate students. He'll be traveling to other Chilean bases along the western side

---

29 http://www.mssu.edu/seg-vm/pict0665.html

30 http://images.google.com/imgres?imgurl=http://principles.ou.edu/grav_ex/worden_photo.jpg&imgrefurl=http://principles.ou.edu/grav_ex/relative.htm&usg=__ekoq2uT9e_hFxyMsietZcqsWH5k=&h=399&w=441&sz=23&hl=en&start=35&um=1&tbnid=mkPezge9HfRfxM:&tbnh=115&tbnw=127&prev=/images%3Fq%3Dgravimeter%26ndsp%3D20%26hl%3Den%26rls%3Dcom.microsoft:en-us%26sa%3DN%26start%3D20%26um%3D1

31 LaCoste-Romberg gravimeters are used for most geodetic work today, although the Worden gravimeters have been used extensively for such work in the past. See: http://earth-info.nga.mil/GandG/publications/geolay/TR80003C.html Worden gravimeters, however, would be sought after as items worthy of being displayed in geoscience museums (if not, perhaps, even used in surveys). In operating conditions, they still could be valued in excess of $13,000 today.

of the Peninsula while I remain at Base Bernardo O'Higgins[32] to help Grant Morris collect rock and fossil samples. But I think this will work to your advantage. Green would be taking it south of our base of operations to such places as Chilean Air Force Base Gabriel González Videla (GGV),[33] which only is occupied during the austral summer."

"That's terrific, Stone. The more data you can gather from different locations along the Peninsula and around the South Shetland Islands, the better."

Ted left with the gravimeter. It would be his constant companion for the next six months. The instrument represented quite a responsibility for a college student, especially one about to embark on a long and perilous journey. *It's worth more than I make in a year as a Research Assistant,* thought Ted; *if anything happens to that instrument, I'm a dead man!*

The quartz gravimeter was mounted inside a bright stainless steel cylindrical housing eighteen inches high and six inches in diameter. Between uses or when transported, it was stored in a padded cylindrical shipping container two feet high and one foot in diameter. By itself, the gravimeter weighed five pounds. The shipping container for the gravimeter was decorated with more than forty decals from Japan, Korea, Taiwan, Hong Kong, Singapore, Macau, Brunei, Indonesia, Papua New Guinea, New Zealand, Australia, India, Pakistan, Iran, Kenya, Egypt, South Africa, Angola, Ghana, Tunisia, Greece, Italy, Crete,

---

32 For a general discussion of Base O'Higgins, see http://en.wikipedia.org/wiki/Puerto_Covadonga. For a photograph of Base O'Higgins, see http://www.antarktis-station.de/. The photograph at the top of the page was taken from a mountain that is located to the south of the base.

33 http://bartosik.org/scrapbook/antarctica/paradise-bay.htm

Cyprus, Spain, France, England, Iceland, Greenland, and other countries. This instrument was a world traveler!

Beginning that day, Ted took readings with the gravimeter at least once a day at the same location, after first visiting the official gravity measurement site at Madison's Dane County Regional Airport. By taking readings daily at the same point, it was possible to determine how the gravimeter's characteristics changed with time. These data, together with the other data collected during the Expedition, would later be used to analyze the data collected in Antarctica.

Ted also instructed David Green in the proper use and care of the instrument.

Of the two graduate students, David appeared to be the more serious. He had a dry sense of humor, if you could get him to talk at all. His fair complexion made him prone to sunburn. This would be a serious problem in the Antarctic during the austral summer because of the intense solar radiation and its reflection off the Continental Glacier. It did not help that few if any effective skin-protection products were available at that time.

When not at the Brittingham Estate, David usually could be found in his laboratory in the basement of Science Hall at the foot of Bascom Hill.[34] "Come in, come in." David waved Ted into his lab with his left hand while adjusting the focus on his microscope with his right. It was close to dinnertime. Ted had stopped by on his way home.

34 http://www.geography.wisc.edu/history/index.htm

"I brought you the itinerary for the trip to Washington, D.C. in October for that Antarctic conference sponsored by the National Science Foundation."

David barely paid attention to what he was saying. "Huh? Oh! Okay." The scientist, over six feet tall, with brown eyes and sandy-colored hair that somehow never looked combed, was dressed in a white lab coat that covered the corduroy pants and open-collared shirt his wife had neatly pressed. David characteristically spent hours peering into a microscope, looking at thin sections of rocks he produced from his rock samples. A threadbare sweater with leather patches lay across a chair, ready for those trips into the chilly autumn air coming off Lake Mendota just to the north of the building. The sweater contained one large hole and several burn marks that had been produced by embers from David's pipe. Smoking it was a crutch he used to help him think through those never-ending problems posed by Nature. A haze of blue smoke hung in the air; it had the sweet smell of his special tobacco blend.

"Could you leave the material on the table? I think I just found what I've been looking for. I need to get over to the shop and cut another thin section from a rock I found on another island. If the two rocks correlate, I'll have a major discovery!"

With that, he ripped off his lab coat, grabbed his sweater, and rushed out the back door. Ted was left to find space on his desk where the itinerary could be placed . . . a spot where it would not get lost among the unfiled correspondence, various reprints, and the last six months of *Geology*[35] that had accumulated while David concentrated on his research.

---

35 *Geology* is the journal of the Geological Society of America

David was married to his high school sweetheart, Alice, so he spent his nights at home. Grant and Ted, on the other hand, who by the fall of 1960 had moved to an apartment they shared on Lake Monona, both had steady girlfriends who attended the University of Wisconsin-Madison. Thus, it was not unusual for Ted and Susan, as well as Grant and his 'steady', Vivian, to study together, either in that apartment or at the University's library. While the ladies delved into school subjects, the men studied material related to Antarctic survival, cold-weather camping, paleontology, gravimetry, and related topics.

Grant, David, and Ted augmented their studies by attending conferences sponsored by the Geophysical and Polar Research Center and various governmental organizations. In October, 1961, for example, the team headed to Washington, DC—or more specifically, to a lodge along the Blue Ridge Parkway and Skyline Drive—for the Annual Conference on Antarctic Studies sponsored by the National Science Foundation's Office of Polar Programs. Lasting a week, the Conference included technical meetings and symposia.

The Foundation had invited scientists from universities, institutions, and research centers across the United States, Europe, Australia, New Zealand, Japan, and other countries that were sending teams to the Antarctic that austral summer. In addition to scientific presentations, the meeting planners scheduled important sessions and outdoor field exercises pertaining to living and surviving in Antarctica.

The topics covered in these sessions and field exercises included dressing for cold-weather field work, surviving wind and temperature extremes, rock climbing, including rappelling from a cliff or, more appropriately, in the case of the Antarctic, from an ice ledge, protecting one's face from the sun as well as its reflection from snow and ice-covered surfaces, and myriad other topics critical to work, health, and survival. Everyone attended these sessions, and even the most experienced attendees took notes.

"Compared to working on ice," commented Rolf Bjornstad one morning, "the climbing and rappelling we'll do today on the side of this cliff will be easy!" Bjornstad was a tall, athletic-looking Norwegian outdoorsman with more than twenty years experience in ice and mountain climbing. He had ten years of experience working in Antarctica with the Norwegian Polar Institute. His face, creased and weather-beaten, with features sculpted by the weather and stress that comes from working under duress, spoke volumes about his knowledge of the environment and the dangers inherent in Antarctic field operations.

"Never forget," he warned the assembled scientists, "Nature *rarely* is forgiving. Once on the continent, you'll have few if any second chances to get it right. In July 1959—" His voice broke. Bjornstad looked down and turned away momentarily before continuing, "My good friend, Dennis 'Tink' Bell, of the British Antarctic Survey fell into a crevasse at Admiralty Bay, King George Island. They never found his body!"[36] [37]

That doesn't sound good, thought Ted. He knew that the University of Wisconsin's team would be working exclusively

36 http://www.antarctica.ac.uk/basclub/deaths.html

37 http://www.antarctic-monument.org/index.php?page=dennis-bell; Memorial: cross in vicinity of base (body not recovered).

in areas near the sea, where the Continental Glacier would be calving[38] throughout the austral summer. The fact that crevasses might open at any time would be a constant threat to their operations, if not to their lives.

"Some of you will be climbing gentle ice slopes—for example, up the Continental Glacier where it slopes down to the sea—so good hiking or mountaineering boots should suffice," Bjornstad continued. "Just make sure they will accommodate crampons[39] in the event you face steeper slopes and need added traction. And for really difficult slopes, an ice axe is a *must.* I'll hold a special class on the tools needed for ice climbing tomorrow morning at 9:00 AM in the main conference hall followed by a special two-hour session on survival and emergency medical treatment at 10:00 AM. I urge you to attend both classes. For today, however, let's work on our rappelling techniques, should you ever face the need to descend from a steep cliff, be it made of rock or ice."

Rappelling down a rock cliff is one thing, thought Ted, as he made his way easily down the side of a sixty-foot cliff behind the lodge. *It's seventy-five degrees, and I'm not wearing a jacket. What's going to happen when the temperature is thirty degrees, I'm dressed in multiple layers of clothing, wearing heavy work shoes and insulated gloves, and making my way out of a crevasse? What then?*

The conference concluded with a dinner in the lodge's Great Hall. T.O. Jones, Head, Office of Antarctic Programs,

---

[38] As glacial ice reaches the sea, pieces break off, or calve, forming icebergs.

[39] Crampons are generally an attachment to outdoor footwear that features metal parts to provide traction on snow and ice. See, for example, http://en.wikipedia.org/wiki/Crampons

National Science Foundation, gave the keynote address for the government.

There's no turning back now, thought Ted. *This is going to be* the *adventure of a lifetime!*

IV
Destination: Santiago

As far as the University of Wisconsin Team was concerned, the Expedition was about to begin! It was Tuesday afternoon in Madison, November 14th. The UW team members, their families, and sweethearts assembled at the Dane County Airport to say good-bye. This was the last time they would see each other until the middle of March, 1962. About a half hour before boarding, Ted explained that he needed to take a set of gravimeter readings. He excused himself and Susan, explaining that she would record the data while he observed it. No one was fooled. Everyone knew it would be their last opportunity to say good-bye . . . one last chance to kiss and embrace.

The flight to Chicago was uneventful, as was their flight to Miami, FL. The large container that held the Worden gravimeter, which occupied a seat by itself between Ted and Grant, never ceased to be the object of questions from other passengers.

"Is it a cookie jar?" some asked, obviously amused with themselves.

"Say, son, could you hand me a beer!"

Ted took it in stride. As good-naturedly as possible, he and Grant attempted to explain exactly what the container held and how the instrument was used. "Let's just say that someday we'll have better maps as a result of the work we're doing," they would say. But it was clear from their glazed-over eyes and the pained expressions on their faces, however, that the other passengers simply did not understand.

Waiting for the team at the terminal in Miami were two friends of Professor O'Mhaille's from the University of Miami's Center for Marine Geology, Professors James Trimble and Michael Granger. Tall, lean, and well-tanned, they epitomized everything Ted had come to envision regarding young, active adults living on the Florida peninsula. *What a life!* he thought. *This sure beats winter in Wisconsin, with those wind chills of -40 degrees and lower! It's enough to make a person switch his college major to tropical marine biology.*

Scooping up everyone's luggage, Trimble and Granger soon had everything packed in their Center's van for the trip to the team's motel.

"We'll see you at 6:00 AM," cried Trimble as he and Granger jumped back into the van after unloading it at the motel. "Be sure to put on your bathing suits and plenty of suntan lotion; it's going to get hot on the water." What they had scheduled was an all day outing of swimming and snorkeling on the reefs off Miami Beach.

Trimble and Granger were waiting at the motel office the next morning at 6:00 AM. With the van loaded, they were off to board the Center's forty-foot inboard cabin cruiser, which was berthed some fifty miles south of Miami. Captain Carpenter was standing on the dock, next to the *Shor-Clif* when they arrived.

"Welcome aboard," he shouted as the six men walked down the pier. "It's a perfect day to be out on the water."

They headed to sea at a moderate ten knots.[40] Professor O'Mhaille and Grant became seasick almost immediately. Both alternated between hanging their heads over the side of the boat and lying on the deck with their eyes closed. The captain suggested in the strongest terms they *not* go below, where they would lose sight of the horizon and, with that, their sense of equilibrium. "Going down there will make things worse, Doc," said the captain, helping Professor O'Mhaille to lie down on a cushion. It was too late for Dramamine, so there was nothing for the professor and Grant to do but "tough it out." The alternative was to cancel the trip, something neither would ask.

Within thirty minutes, the *Shor-Clif* reached the first reef. With David and Ted behind them, Professors Trimble and Granger jumped off the side of the boat and headed to the bottom. The view was unlike anything that Ted had seen. He was totally overwhelmed, by the reef as well as the abundant fish swimming in and among the coral beds, to see the school of young barracuda[41] bearing down on him from behind. Known for their fang-like teeth, large pointed heads with an under bite, and general fearsome appearance, the sight of the first barracuda passing over his head was enough to make Ted wonder why he even agreed to go on the outing. He crouched low to the reef and held perfectly still until the entire school passed. Then, he made for surface as quickly as his flippers could push him there. David and the two University of Miami professors followed.

---

40 The knot is a unit of speed equal to one nautical mile per hour; it is equal to 1.151 miles per hour

41 http://en.wikipedia.org/wiki/Barracuda

Once they all had reached the surface, Professor Trimble took off his snorkel mask, shook the water out of his hair, and started laughing. "You don't have to worry about them, Ted. They're scavengers!"

Professor Granger and David were laughing as well. "Don't be deceived by any preconceived notions you might have, Ted. They rarely, if ever, have been known to attack swimmers," continued Granger, now laughing so hard that he started coughing.

Rarely, if ever, attack swimmers, thought Ted . . . *that's good to know. Oh, hell, you can't live forever. If the water's safe enough for the likes of Trimble, Granger, and David, it's okay for me.*

"Thanks, guys. I appreciate you telling me this *now!"* said Ted, joining in their amusement.

The time was 2:30 AM, the date, November 17th. The aircraft was ready. It had been a hectic three days in Miami, full of diving, sightseeing, and several seminars conducted by the Center for Marine Geology. Now, it was time to push on to South America.

With the last passengers boarded, the aircraft taxied onto the runway. At 3:00 AM, engines revved, the captain released the brakes, and the Panagra DC-8 roared down the runway, its destination: Panama.

Shortly after 6:00 AM, the plane touched down at Panama's Tocumen International Airport. Ted left the aircraft with his gravimeter to take some readings and stretch his legs. The air was steamy—stifling, in fact—with the temperature already in the low nineties. With the plane refueled, it flew to Guayaquil. Here, the time on the ground was barely sufficient for Ted to acquire the gravimeter readings he needed. Then, it was back on the plane for the final leg of their flight to Lima.

What a way to make a living, thought Ted. He knew from conversations that he had with others in the Department of Geology and Geophysics that Professor Woollard had several full-time employees whose job it was to travel year-round for the sole purpose of taking gravimeter readings at airports and other sites worldwide. *I'll bet they have some stories to tell.*

The team was met at Lima's International Airport by a long-time friend and colleague of Professor O'Mhaille's, Professor Victor Martinez, of the University of Peru's Department of Geology.

To Ted, Lima was unlike anything he had experienced. He was struck by the contrasts. In the poorer areas on the outskirts, people lived in small huts constructed of mud and straw. Inhabitants could be seen urinating in the streets, suggesting a total lack of public sanitation facilities and personal hygiene. On the other hand, he found the center of the city as cosmopolitan as any major city found in North America.

Once the men had checked into a small, inexpensive hotel in the center of the downtown business district, they went to lunch at the estate of a friend of Professor Martinez's. The estate overlooked the ocean in Miraflores, an upscale district of Lima. Situated on several acres of finely manicured lawn, it was completely enclosed, for security purposes, by a high brick wall. Three servants attended to everyone's needs during the five-course meal while two other servants attended to the host's three young children.

The conversation was polite but guarded. There was no mention of politics, the disparity between the classes, or anything that might in the least bit controversial. Nor should there have been. This was, after all, a visit among friends—professionals, at that—and matters other than science and family were not proper topics for discussion.

It was not until the team and Professor Martinez were back in the car that the subject of the economy and lack of a middle class came up.

"You must understand," said Martinez, "the inflation in our country is 9%.[42] Unless you are born to wealth or are a military officer or government official, it is difficult, if not impossible, to improve your lot in life. Making things worse is the fact that those who *do* have money will *not* invest it here. They prefer to keep their wealth in *alternative* 'investments,' things like U.S. dollars, gold and silver coins and bars, foreign securities, and jewelry.

"I'll bet you a Brazilian 20,000 Reis gold coin, Ethan, that if we could peer into the safe deposit boxes in the Banco Central de Reserva del Perú in Lima, they would be loaded with everything *but* our currency and stock certificates from Peruvian corporations! And what's there would be only a fraction of this country's wealth. Most of *that* is held in the vaults of major financial institutions in New York, London, and Paris.

---

42 http://www.iadb.org/res/centralBanks/publications/cbm39_255.pdf (see table, page 6)

"Believe me," Martinez continued, "if there's a way for someone—*anyone*—in my country to beg, borrow, or steal an extra sol,[43] *by any means*, they will do it!"

I guess that explains the extra 'tax' that appeared on our breakfast bill this morning, thought Professor O'Mhaille as Martinez drove up to the team's hotel.

The flight to Santiago on November 21st was without incident, and provided a good opportunity for everyone to catch up on their sleep. The days in Lima had been well spent visiting sites of geologic interest as well as pre-Inca and Inca ruins. Now, it was time for Professor O'Mhaille, Morris, and Green to refresh their knowledge of Chilean geology before the team pushed farther south to the Strait of Magellan and Tierra del Fuego.

Their host was Professor Alejandro Barría, one of the most renowned geologists and seismologists in North and South America. Dr. Barría was a Professor Emeritus in the Department of Geology and Geophysics at the University of Chile. He had arranged rooms for the party at the Hotel Emperador, in the heart of Santiago. The hotel was on the main thoroughfare through the center of the city, Avenida Libertador Bernardo O'Higgins. Santiago's main avenue, it runs east-west in the center of the greater urban area, is nine miles long, and has

43 Due to high inflation the currency of Republican Peru, the Sol, was abandoned in 1985 and the Inti introduced. Caused by the bad economic state of Peru and terrorism in the late 1980s, the Inti soon lost its value as well, hyperinflation struck the country, and the Peruvian government was forced to introduce a new currency in 1991: the Nuevo Sol. http://www.limaeasy.com/money/peruvian_money.php

five lanes in each direction. It was named after Chile's founding father, Bernardo O'Higgins.

During the day, Professor Barría and his students hosted field trips to the south of Santiago as well as to the west, along the Pacific coast. Highlights included stops at Farellones, El Volcán, Viña del Mar, Concón, and Valparaiso. Field excursions were important to Ted because they provided opportunities for him to hone skills as a field geologist, something that would be a great importance once the UW team "hit the ice."

On some occasions, evenings were spent with Dr. Barría at some of Santiago's finer restaurants, followed by a movie or a floor show. Other times, when Señor Joaquín Covas hosted the UW team, the entertainment appealed more to a person's "baser" instincts. It featured burlesque and strip tease performances.

Tall and thin with blond hair and blue eyes, Joaquín, single, was quite the ladies' man. He could always find an excuse for a good night on the town. Joaquín spoke flawless English, so conversation came easily. When he hosted the UW scientists in Santiago, everyone always found it difficult to wake up the next morning in time for the start of the day's field trip.

It was not until one evening's festivities lasted well into the following morning, 2:00 AM, to be exact, and on a weeknight, no less, that Professor O'Mhaille suggested to Grant and Ted—David usually spent his evening reading scientific journals—they might want to consider a more reasonable time to end their evenings' festivities. "Come on, guys," he urged them the next morning as Grant dozed off for the second time during breakfast, "the least you can do is try to stay awake during the day, and especially when we're out in the field. The last thing I need is for one of you two to fall asleep and roll off a cliff while we're out there collecting rock samples! I'm too old to rappel down a cliff and haul you to the top! Besides, my back simply can't take it!"

Joaquín was an employee of the University of Chile's Department of Geology and Geophysics. It was his job to ensure that the equipment needed by the University's scientists was assembled and shipped to the Fleet Warehouse in Punta Arenas in time for the Expedition's departure. He also would be traveling to Punta Arenas with the scientists. There, his job would be to resolve any last-minute problems that arose regarding clothing and equipment. Both Grant and Ted were looking forward to seeing him there. From what they had heard, there was not much to do in the city, and the last thing they wanted to do was sit in a hotel room, staring at four walls! With Covas in town, that was *not* likely to happen.

By December 2nd, it was time to leave Santiago. There would be a farewell party for the University of Wisconsin scientists later that evening hosted by the University of Chile's Department of Geology and Geophysics. In the meantime, Ted busied himself taking gravimeter readings on the sidewalk in front of the hotel. Initial analyses indicated that the gravimeter's quartz mechanism had been 'drifting' smoothly with time since the team left Madison, an important finding that portended good results on his return to Madison. However well things might have gone up to now, though, Ted knew that it would not be long before the *real* work would begin. With it would come increased dangers and all the risks associated with working in the Antarctic, regardless of the season.

V

Punta Arenas, Chile: Gateway to Antarctica

Punta Arenas; a more desolate place Ted had never seen. It was late in the afternoon on December 3rd when the plane from Santiago set down. For the first time in his life he was homesick. The area around the airport was flat, with hard-packed ground, scrub grass, and small trees, most of which did not even come up to his shoulders. He thought about Susan and his family, and of where they might be, of what they might be doing at that very moment. And he pictured the gently rolling fields and tall trees found in southern Wisconsin and along the shores of Lake Michigan, beautiful even after the leaves had fallen. *What* am *I doing here?*

While not the southernmost population center in the world—Puerto Williams, Chile, and Ushuaia, Argentina, to the south of Punta Arenas, are smaller—Punta Arenas is, because of its size, considered the southernmost *city* in the world.[44] It lies on the Strait of Magellan and long has served as an important port, even after the advent of the Panama Canal. Its population is largely of Croatian and Spanish descent, with smaller numbers of Germans, English, Italians, and Swiss. The architecture is

44 http://en.wikipedia.org/wiki/Punta_Arenas

largely European, as is the culture. Oil and sheep are the two most important commodities associated with port trade, and the large sheep ranges to the north of the city attract livestock buyers from around the world.

The UW scientists as well as some forty other passengers on the plane waited inside the terminal while the bus to the city was loaded by the driver and the airport manager. It took thirty minutes. Finally, the airport manager came into the terminal and announced, *"El autobús está cargado, mis amigos."*[45] When everyone got outside, they were dumbfounded. There, atop the bus, was all of the passengers' luggage—every last suitcase, duffle bag, cardboard box, what-have-you—stacked four feet high and held in place with ropes tied to fasteners just below the roof line.

Now the question was, how was the driver, once the bus was underway, going to get everything to the passengers' destination, the Hotel Cosmos? Certainly, the suitcases at the very top of the pile were perched at precarious angles! And the road to town was unsurfaced and full of potholes. It presented constant obstacles. Yet, by slowing to a crawl, the driver managed to deliver passengers and cargo to the hotel just as darkness descended.

The innkeeper already had lit a fire in the hotel's huge fireplace, and the burning logs provided both light and a warm welcome. The hotel was a major gathering point in the city and home to the Rotary Club. It was a large square-shaped, three-story structure with a courtyard in the middle. Constructed completely of wood, the first floor housed the service counter, several offices, the kitchen, a large restaurant, multiple storage

---

45 "The bus is loaded, my friends."

areas, and several guest rooms. The second and third floors were primarily devoted to guest quarters.

The courtyard was largely unused and devoid of anything but hard-packed earth, with a few shrubs growing here and there. It was home to a flock of chickens, which Ted soon surmised were being kept both for their eggs as well as their meat. In the days to come he also observed sheep buyers from England who stayed at the hotel using small air-powered BB guns—toys, really, that were purchased at a little shop across the street from the hotel—to shoot at the chickens from the second-floor windows of their rooms, which overlooked the courtyard. While the BBs never did anything except annoy the chickens, the use of the little guns *did* have the effect of relieving the sheep-buyers' boredom.

Ted took the necessary gravimeter readings the next morning at the base of the stairs of the Port Administration Building,[46] the designated Punta Arenas gravity site. The data were needed to refine the *difference* in the pull of gravity between Punta Arenas and Santiago. Just as important, the reading taken in Punta Arenas would serve as the starting point for the new gravity network to be established in the Chilean Antarctic.

It did not take long for *La Prensa Austral*, Punta Arenas's newspaper, to begin coverage of the Expedition and its participants. A major article published on December 21, 1961 featured a story on Chilean naval personnel who would be participating, their ships, and the mission of the Expedition. Published was information on civilian personnel accompanying

---

46 Theodore J. Cohen, "Gravity Survey of Chilean Antarctic Bases," Journal of Geophysical Research, Volume 68, Number 1, Washington, D.C., January 1, 1963

the military contingent, including the University of Chile and University of Wisconsin scientists. After the article was published, Professor O'Mhaille, Grant, David, and Ted were recognized wherever they traveled in and around the city.

The *Lientur* arrived mid-day on December 4th, and the UW team was invited aboard by Captain Muñoz for a field trip down the Strait of Magellan into Tierra del Fuego,[47] the Land of Fire. An archipelago, the region, with its snow-topped mountains and glaciers, is spectacular. It reminds many of the Aleutian Islands, Iceland, the Alaskan Peninsula, and the Faroe Islands.[48]

From time to time, Captain Muñoz anchored in a protective cove and ordered his men to lower a motorized launch into the water. *"Doctor O'Mhaille, mis hombres están a su servicio. Ellos lo llevarán a usted y a sus científicos adondequiera que usted desee ir.*[49] Please, how can we be of service to you?" In this way, the UW scientists were able to explore the geology of several islands within the archipelago, a unique experience and one for which they were grateful. These stops also afforded opportunities for the team to gather rock samples that Grant, in particular, later would use in his thesis to demonstrate a close geologic link between the tip of South America and the North Antarctic Peninsula.

The *Lientur* returned to Punta Arenas early on December 8th. With the weather cold, wet, and windy, there was little to do

47 http://en.wikipedia.org/wiki/Tierra_del_Fuego
48 See footnote 47
49 "Doctor O'Mhaille, the men are at your service. They will take you and your scientists wherever you want to go."

but stay in the hotel and read. It also was a good time to write letters home.

"Eduardo. Eduardo! We need to talk!" It was Lucero, who had just returned to the *Lientur* after having spent the afternoon at the Fleet Warehouse. He whispered the words as he walked past Bellolio toward the stairs leading to the deck below. "Meet me at the bulkhead behind the engine room in five minutes."

Bellolio nodded. Spotting a petty officer standing on the deck above him, he shouted, "De Stefano, take over! I'm needed below."

Once below deck, and after making to sure they were alone, Lucero began talking in a low voice. "I offered to help Chief Warrant Officer Zalazar, who works in the Fleet Warehouse, with an inventory of the freight to be loaded on the *Piloto Pardo* for the Expedition. We have been crawling all over the warehouse since the *Lientur* arrived in port today. I tell you, Eduardo, I'm too old for this. I only did it for one reason. I needed to find our refrigerator. I had to see the crate with my own eyes, to check out the reinforcing pine strips and strapping. I wanted to make sure no one had opened the box!"

"Well, did you find it?"

"Take a look." Lucero pulled the Expedition's manifest for the *Piloto Pardo* from his back pocket and flipped the pages to page six. There, he pointed to lines 317A and B.

317A	Refrigerador	1SGT Leonardo Rodríguez	O'Higgins
317B	Arica	Via Punta Arenas	B27-M43

"I'm telling you, Eduardo, our Navy's transportation and warehousing system is a modern miracle. Give me a typewriter and I can move anything, anywhere, anytime!"

"And?" Bellolio was looking him straight in the eye, his voice now considerably louder than a whisper. "And?"

"Shhhhhh! Keep your voice down! The crate is fine! No one's so much as touched a nail!

"I also took advantage of the military telephone system to make a call," Lucero continued, "all official like, mind you, to Rodríguez at Army Headquarters in Santiago. He was attending some class or something. I wanted to let him know that because him and me was such great buddies, and because I already was down here with the *Lientur,* I bought him a refrigerator as my gift to him and his family. Well, he got all blubbery on me, so I didn't stay on the line with him long. But I just told him that, because we went back so far and was such good friends, it was the least I could do for him. And besides, I says, I got no family. Then I asked him, 'What else am I gonna do with my money?'

"Besides, Eduardo, I didn't want him getting down here and buying something locally. That would really cause a problem, especially when both the Army and the Navy informed him that he already had something in the Fleet Warehouse. How would *that* look when he asked them what the hell they was talking about?"

"You didn't tell him *I* was involved, did you?" asked Bellolio.

"Oh, no, Eduardo. No sense confusing the man. Besides, he don't know you. And God forbid, if anything went wrong and someone got wind of what was in that crate, I sure would hate for you to be dragged into the mess. It's probably best, for now, that you remain . . . ah, what do they call people like you . . . ah, yes, a 'silent partner.' The less people what knows about you, Eduardo, the better."

In southern Chile, the weather changed two or three times a day, every day, going from sunny, to windy and rainy, and back to sunny again. To Ted, it seemed as if the winds always were blowing at twenty to thirty miles per hour, sometimes higher. Navy personnel stationed in the city told him the winds actually were strongest during the austral summer and, in fact, the highest recorded wind speed in Punta Arenas during that time of year was eighty miles per hour. At least it was 'warm'. During the summer, temperatures in the city climbed as high as 57 degrees. *Just our luck. All we've experienced our entire time down here is cold, rainy, and windy weather!*

"Everyone into the taxi!" shouted Joaquín as he leaped through the front door into the lobby of the Cosmos Hotel. "We're going to Lucy's!"

Never mind that it was 11:00 PM. Professor O'Mhaille, Grant, and Ted were reading in the hotel's lobby. David had gone upstairs to take a shower and retire to bed early. Grant started up the stairs. "I better get David up. He'll never forgive us if we leave him behind."

"And I better go along with you to Lucy's to make sure you gents don't get into trouble," O'Mhaille deadpanned. "The last thing we need is an international incident that affects Chilean-American relations!"

"Oh, yes, of course," said Grant, in mock concern. "We couldn't have that happen. Think what the headline in tomorrow's newspaper might read: 'Professor and Students from University of Wisconsin Involved in Incident at House of Prostitution'."

"One thing before we leave," warned Joaquín, "be sure to take only a little paper money with you, and put that in your shoes. Leave your wallets in the hotel's safe! The ladies, if you can call them that, are expert pickpockets. They wouldn't hesitate to take every cent you have. They could care less if you even have enough money for taxi fare back to the hotel."

With everyone in the taxi, they sped off for the city's Red Light District. Lucy's, one of the oldest and certainly the most famous house of ill repute in all of Punta Arenas, was housed in a nondescript two-story building about ten minutes from the port. Joaquín paid the driver, and the five men entered the building. They were greeted by the madam. She showed them into the dance hall and motioned for a young girl to take their drink orders.

The dance hall, on the first floor, was roughly sixty feet long and thirty feet wide. The ceiling was covered with mirrors while the walls, from floor to ceiling, were papered with red velveteen. There were doors along the two longest walls, six doors to the wall, fitted flush with the walls.

It took only a moment before five doors along one wall opened. In walked five flashily dressed and perfumed prostitutes. Each had done her makeup and hair to perfection, was dressed in a gown of a bright solid color with underlying crinoline,[50] and wore high-heeled shoes. One by one, each took

50 Crinolines are still worn today. They are usually part of a formal outfit, such as an evening gown or a wedding dress. The volume of the skirt is not as great as during the Victorian era, so modern crinolines are most often constructed of several layers of stiff net, with flounces to extend the skirt. See: http://en.wikipedia.org/wiki/Crinoline

a man by the hand and led him to the dance floor for a spirited and provocative dance to the heavy beat of recorded Latin American music.

The professor breathed a sigh of relief when the first dance ended, took a handkerchief out of his pocket, and wiping his brow, accepted the drink he had ordered from the young girl. The men offered their dance partners drinks, but from the women's hand gestures and what they said in Spanish, there was no doubt that it was against House rules for the young women to drink while they 'worked.'

The room soon began filling with other men from the community, which only brought more flashily dressed women to the dance floor from rooms on either side of the hall. Lucy's and the other 'houses' in the District were an integral part of the city's night life, and men came not only for sex, but for drinking and dancing as well.

Joaquín and his charges barely had time to catch their breaths when the music started again. With the girls tugging at their arms, off they went to the dance floor. The cycle repeated itself three times. Finally, the professor, with one hand on his back and a sheepish look on his face, turned to Grant and remarked, "I've had enough dancing for one evening. I'm going to take a taxi back to the hotel and turn in." Given the nature of the situation, Grant, David, and Ted thought it best to join him.

Joaquín laughed. "*¡Ustedes norteamericanos no tienen idea de como divertirse!*[51] Go on, I'll pay the bar bill. We'll catch up in the morning."

---

51 "You Americans don't know how to have a good time!"

When they left, Joaquín was in the arms of a beautiful young brunette with fiery black eyes—the one dressed in a bright red gown—who could not keep her hands off him.

U.S. Air Force Captain Frank Lawson registered at the hotel late one evening. Ted was sitting just across from the hotel's front desk, reading by the fire. He could not help overhearing the captain talk to the night clerk as he registered.

He saw Lawson an hour later, when the captain returned to the lobby from his room, now dressed in civilian clothes. Ted introduced himself and asked him if he would like to join him at a table in the corner of the hotel's dining room for dinner. "Of course, lead the way," said Lawson with a smile.

Lawson was a tall man with sharp features, black hair that was block-cut with a tapered appearance, obviously regulation, and a disarming Southern manner. He and Ted fell into conversation easily. It was not long before they were talking about everything from jobs, to family, to the game of chess.

Frank and his crew had flown into Punta Arenas that afternoon from the Panama Canal Zone, just another flight on what to Lawson seemed a never-ending string of flights that had taken them from the United States, to South America, South Africa, and back again. All were intended to deliver the personnel and equipment needed at the many ground monitoring and precision tracking sites under construction as part of NASA's Mercury and Apollo space programs.[52] [53]

Frank had not seen his family since May. To make matters worse, he had to leave his wife a week before his second child

52 http://www-pao.ksc.nasa.gov/kscpao/history/mercury/mercury.htm
53 http://www.nasm.si.edu/collections/imagery/Apollo/apollo.htm

was born. *People who are not in the military, or who don't have family members in the military,* thought Ted, *must have a difficult time understanding the sacrifices these people make every day of their lives.*

But Frank was not complaining, just stating facts. And while his schedule was tight, his spirits were buoyed by the fact that he now was scheduled to return to his home in Florida, where he was based, before the end of the year.

The men finished their dinner, whereupon Frank challenged Ted to a game of chess in the lobby before they turned in for the night. Frank brought his board and chess box down from his room, and the two men placed the pieces on the board.

"What'll it be, captain, heads or tails?"

Lawson chose 'heads' and won the toss. Taking White, he had the honor of making the first move. Before starting the game, however, he paused, looked at Ted, and said with a grin, "I guess in all fairness I should tell you something. I was the Southeastern United States Chess Champion every year from 1955 through 1959. Things got a little busy for me after that."

Ted smiled. "Well, I guess you're going to teach me some great new strategies this evening, Captain."

In the first game, after bringing his White *knights* out on the second and third moves and having watched Ted's moves in Black, Lawson sat back in his chair and cried, "Ah ha! This is starting to look like the game between Fischer and Petrosian in the 1959 matches held in Belgrade, Yugoslavia![54] Unfortunately, if we continue this way, I'm going to have to bring my *queen* out early!" Ted was amazed that he had the time to follow the

54 http://www.worldchesslinks.net/ezde2.html

World Chess Championships, much less commit major matches to memory.

Maybe he gets a lot of time to read when he's on the ground and socked in by weather, thought Ted. *Whatever he does, it seems to work for him!*

When they finally finished playing at 2:30 AM, the score was 3-1 in Frank's favor; they agreed to a draw on one game. Ted thought Frank's playing was nothing less than amazing. He would make a move, then, from time to time, cite a game in which the move he had just made had been crucial to a famous player's winning strategy.

"Nice try with that 'poisoned pawn' deception[55] in the third game," said Frank, smiling, as the two men returned the chess pieces to their box. "For just a moment I thought it was a blunder. Then I saw what you were doing. But it did give me pause and force me to readjust my game."

"Right," said Ted. "And all the while, you're schmoozing[56] me with your Southern drawl and polite conversation, hoping to lull me into some false sense of security while you plan surreptitiously to swoop down and capture whatever piece may be threatening you at the time! I was on to you, Captain!"

Lawson let out a belly laugh. He truly enjoyed the evening and its challenges, as did Ted. "I would hope that someday we

---

55 The Poisoned Pawn Variation is any of several chess opening variations where a pawn is said to be 'poisoned' because its capture can result in positional problems or material loss for the captor. The best-known of these, and that most often described as the "Poisoned Pawn Variation," is a line of the Sicilian Defense, Najdorf Variation. See, for example, http://en.wikipedia.org/wiki/Poisoned_Pawn_Variation

56 To converse casually, especially in order to gain an advantage or make a social connection. See, for example, http://www.thefreedictionary.com/schmoozing

will have a rematch," he exclaimed as they climbed the stairs to the hotel's second floor.

Regrettably, because Lawson was to fly his transport to the Union of South Africa at 11:00 AM that morning and would not return to Punta Arenas for several weeks, the two men never saw each other again.

Except for the international mail, an infrequent source of communications from the United States directed to the UW team through the University of Chile, the only other means of communications with people at home were telephone and Amateur radio. The former was far too expensive, leaving only Amateur radio.

More popularly known as 'ham radio', Amateur radio was a hobby that Ted had practiced since he took his first set of exams for a Novice license before a federal examiner in Milwaukee, Wisconsin, at the age of thirteen. If he could somehow find an Amateur station in Punta Arenas, the possibility was good that he could get messages to Susan and his parents.

Ted asked questions around town regarding who might own and operate such a station, but no one knew of anyone. Then, by chance, on a walk around the better part of town one afternoon, he spotted what appeared to be a fifty-foot tower in the back yard of a large mansion. The tower was topped off with a 3-element Yagi-Uda array[57] for the 10-, 15-, and 20-meter Amateur bands!

Ted could barely contain himself. He took the stairs leading to the porch two at a time, rang the bell, and waited. It did not

57 http://en.wikipedia.org/wiki/Yagi_antenna

take long for a maid to open the door. She was a short woman, dressed entirely in white from her shoes to the small headpiece pinned to her hair. She spoke no English.

"¿En que le puedo servir, señor?"[58]

"Mi nombre es Señor Stone. Yo soy un científico en la XVI° Epedición Chilena a la Antártica. Yo vi que tiene una torre con antena de radio detrás de su casa. ¿Está el radio aficionado en casa?"[59]

"No señor, lo siento mucho. Él está en su trabajo ahora pero regresará mañana. Si es usted tan amable de regresar mañana a las 1500 horas yo le diré que usted vendrá."[60]

"¡Gracias! Volveré mañana. Por favor dígale que se lo agradezco."[61] said Ted.

At exactly 3:00 PM the next afternoon, Ted, Professor O'Mhaille, and David—Grant was in the field with some of the scientists from the University of Chile—arrived at the radio operator's home and rang the bell. The maid opened the door, immediately recognized Ted, and after greeting the guests, ushered them into the ham shack.

"Mi patrón tuvo que trabajar hoy, desafortunadamente, pero él me dijo que usted puede usar su estación de radio, GE8AG, el tiempo que sea necesario y le desea buena suerte

---

58 "How may I be of service to you, sir?"

59 "My name is Mister Stone. I am a scientist with the 16th Chilean Expedition to the Antarctic. I saw the antenna on the tower in the backyard. Is the radio operator at home?"

60 "No, sir, I am so sorry. He is at work right now. But he will be home tomorrow, so if you would be so kind as to return around 1500 hours, I will tell him to expect you."

61 "Thank you! I will return tomorrow. And please thank the operator as well."

para que pueda comunicarse con sus colegas de los Estados Unidos.”[62]

Ted thanked her and took a seat in front of the equipment, with which he was *not* familiar. However, the receiver and transmitter had been manufactured in the United States by the Collins Radio Company[63]. They were not unlike most equipment of their day. Even without the manuals, it took Ted little time to tune the transmitter and receiver to the 20-meter phone band. This band is situated in the middle of the shortwave spectrum,[64] at frequencies better suited for long-distance communications and where atmospheric noise is almost non-existent. With the antenna turned toward the United States, he put out a call for anyone who could either run a phone patch[65] to Madison and Milwaukee, WI or pass messages to people in those cities.

Radio conditions were abysmal! This was not the first time that Ted had fought the ionosphere. He had been a licensed Amateur radio operator for nine years and he knew that conditions varied from day to day, even from hour to hour. He knew he might not be successful, but he also knew that he

---

62 “My employer was called in to work today, unfortunately, but he asks that you use his station, CE8AG, as much as necessary, and he wishes you good luck on reaching your parties in the United States.”

63 The Collins Radio Company of Cedar Rapids, Iowa, was started by Arthur Collins. As a young ham radio operator in high school (call sign : 9CXX (SK)), Collins was in daily contact with the Navy’s 1925 Arctic Expedition to the North Pole led by Commander D.B. MacMillian. See, for example, http://rockwellcollinsmuseum.org/aa_collins/aac_story.php. Note that when an amateur radio operator passes away, his code key is said to have gone silent, and so, he is referred to as a silent key, with (SK) appended to his or her call sign.

64 The shortwave spectrum extends from 3.0 to 30.0 MHz. It also is known as the high-frequency (HF) band.

65 A phone patch ties the radio receiver into the telephone line, enabling the party on the telephone to listen and talk to the party on the radio.

and the others had nothing to lose! And the conditions always could change.

Call after call went out. Sooner or later, he hoped, someone would pick up his signal.

It took over two hours of calling before finally . . . *finally* . . . a station in New Jersey responded. Barely audible at first, the signals on both ends slowly built in strength until they were of the highest quality.

In short order, Ted was talking directly to Susan for the first time since the team left Miami. When they finished, the operator in New Jersey called the Stone household in Milwaukee, and Ted talked with his mother. Then, Professor O'Mhaille and David, in turn, talked to their wives. The afternoon buoyed everyone's spirits, both in Punta Arenas and in the States. On the way back to the hotel late that afternoon, the team stopped at a florist shop and sent a large bouquet of roses to the radio operator's home together with a note, thanking him for his generosity.

By December 15th, the *Piloto Pardo* and the *Yelcho* had arrived in Punta Arenas. Over the last several days, the ships had made their way south from Puerto Montt into the Gulf of Corcovado, down through the Chonos Archipelago, and south through the islands off the west coast of Chile to the Strait of Magellan, finally arriving in Punta Arenas, a long and arduous voyage and one without alternatives.

Loading these vessels began immediately upon their docking in the city's harbor. Traffic in and around the streets nearest the port, including the one in front of the Hotel

Cosmos, was snarled almost constantly throughout the day. Soldiers, sailors, and airmen, both enlisted men and officers, were seen on the streets and in the shops of the city well into the late evening hours.

Those military personnel who had not already made their purchases were hurriedly acquiring luxury foreign-built appliances that, upon shipment to and from the Antarctic, would be exempted from the otherwise high import duties levied by the Chilean government on such items. Once payment had been made and the official paperwork completed and signed, it was the merchant's job to deliver the sealed crates to the Dock Master by the date and time previously specified by the Navy. This was necessary so that the freight could be logged into the Fleet Warehouse and subsequently loaded for the voyage south.

Other than Chief Warrant Officer Lucero and Chief Petty Officer Bellolio, no one paid attention to one particular crate that was moved from the Fleet Warehouse to the *Piloto Pardo* late on the evening prior to the flotilla's departure for the Antarctic. It was the crate containing the refrigerator 'purchased' by Chilean Army First Sergeant Leonardo Rodríguez the previous year in Talcahuano. The crate's destination: Base Bernardo O'Higgins, the Chilean Antarctic. Lucero, who had volunteered to work on the *Piloto Pardo* during the loading of the vessel, personally directed its placement in the ship's hold. Nothing, *absolutely nothing*, was going to be left to chance when it came to the safe transport of this valuable cargo to Antarctica!

Lucero, who had volunteered to work on the *Piloto Pardo* during the loading of the vessel, personally directed the placement of Rodríguez's crate in the ship's hold.[66]

66 Photo by author

VI
The Shrieking Sixties: Crossing the Drake Passage

By December 21, 1961, all was in readiness for the voyage south. The cold-weather clothing, survival kits, field rations, and scientific tools the University of Wisconsin team would need for the next four months had been shipped ahead and now were aboard the *Piloto Pardo.* The ship was built in Holland and named for Luis Alberto Pardo Villalón,[67] the acting commander of the former Chilean tugboat *S.S. Yelcho* that rescued Ernest Shackleton when he returned to Elephant Island from his ill-fated expedition to Antarctica in 1917.[68] [69] The *Piloto Pardo,* which had two light helicopters on her aft deck, was specifically configured for Antarctic service.

67 In Chile, people bear two surnames and a name. The first surname is the paternal surname; the second is the maternal surname. The persons name is either simple or composite; the second part is not a middle name. In the example here, "Luis Alberto Pardo Villalón", he would be known as Luis Pardo. (There are exceptions to this rule, or course.)

68 http://www.victory-cruises.com/antarctic_dreams_history.html

69 http://www.antarctic-circle.org/llag.ship.htm#050

She would serve as the Commodore's flagship for the duration of the Expedition.[70] [71]

The ship currently named *Yelcho* was the former *USS Tekesta*, *Navajo*-class fleet tug built during World War II for the United States Navy.[72] She was intended to serve as a utility ship for the Expedition. She also would serve as a transport ship for scientists and military personnel who needed to be moved among the various offshore research sites as well as among the Chilean and U.S. bases in the South Shetland Islands and on the North Antarctic Peninsula.

The *Lientur* was built during World War II for the United States Navy and later was transferred to the Chilean Navy in 1947.[73] She also was intended to serve as a utility ship for the Expedition, providing both general fleet support as well as transporting scientists and military personnel among the Chilean bases and work sites on the North Antarctic Peninsula.

Looking at the *Piloto Pardo, the Yelcho,* and the *Lientur* from the deck of the *Piloto Pardo,* one thought crept into Ted's mind: *they make a formidable expeditionary force indeed.* He and the members of the Expedition soon would learn, however, that Man, regardless of the size of his ships and the preparations he made, is

---

70 The *Piloto Pardo* was 272 feet long and 39 feet wide, and was capable of cruising at 12 knots . See http://www.antarctic.cl/web_eng/nuestro_barco_historia.php

71 Today, the *Piloto Pardo* is know as the *Antarctic Dream* and serves as an Antarctic passenger vessel. http://www.antarctic.cl/web_eng/nuestro_barco_tecnica.php

72 The *Yelcho* was transferred to the Chilean Navy in 1960. Exactly 205 feet long and 38.5 feet wide, she had a top speed of 16.5 knots . See http://en.wikipedia.org/wiki/USS_Tekesta_(AT-93)

73 The *Lientur* was 143 feet long and 34 feet wide, and had a top speed of 13 knots. Ibid.

no match for Nature on the High Seas. This is especially so in the waters of the Drake Passage and the Bransfield Strait.

The Expedition left the harbor in Punta Arenas at 8:00 PM local time on December 21st, with the *Piloto Pardo* in the lead, followed by the *Lientur* and the *Yelcho*, in that order.[74] Before embarking, Ted had taken one last set of gravimeter readings in Punta Arenas at the Port Administration Building. The gravimeter then was safely stowed aboard the *Piloto Pardo* for the voyage south.

The three ships slowly pulled away from the dock to the cheers and waves of the few family members and friends who had made the trip to Punta Arenas to see the Expedition off. Once out of the harbor, the flotilla moved down the Strait of Magellan at twelve knots. As scientists, the UW contingent was provided with its own quarters, a room containing four bunks just off the infirmary. Chilean Air Force and Army officers also were provided with quarters. Enlisted men from the Chilean Air Force and Army slept on cots placed in the passageways.

By 10:00 PM local time, the sun set, staying below the horizon until 2:30 AM the following morning. The farther south the Expedition travelled, the shorter were the nights. By the time the flotilla reached its area of operations off the Antarctic Peninsula, the sun would only dip briefly below the horizon before rising again, forcing everyone to live by their watches. There simply was no other way to know when to rise, eat, work, or go to sleep.

74 Buques de la Flotilla Antartica Zarparan con Destino a la Region Polar a las 20 Horas de Hoy, "La Prensa Austral," Punta Arenas, Jueves, 21 de Diciembre de 1961

Ted enjoyed the nights and early morning hours best. The ship was quiet, and almost everyone was asleep.

"Teodoro, come on in . . . the radio shack is yours!" It was Marco, the duty communications officer. If the men in the radio shack had no official Fleet traffic to pass during the night, they often would retune the ship's large World War II-era BC-610 600-Watt transmitter for the 20-meter ham band. Once all was in readiness, they would let Ted send messages to Susan and his family via ham operators in the States using the ship's Amateur radio callsign, CE9AW/MM.[75]

Ted also relished the challenge the radiomen posed to him on the morning of the second day out as well as at other times during the voyage: "Copy, if you can, Teodoro, *without error,* what is being broadcast in International Morse code to the Fleet from Naval Headquarters in Santiago at 3:00 AM local time."

The broadcasts, unencrypted transmissions in Spanish, always were sent at forty words per minute.[76] "We will use our typewriters, Teodoro," said Marco, grinning, as he took his seat next to Silva, a junior-grade enlisted operator. Their copy was perfect. But because Ted was forced to use pencil and paper, he could only copy about five minutes at a time before his mind started to slip behind what was being transmitted.[77] Ted *never* won a competition.

---

75 The "/MM" designation following the callsign is used to indicate a maritime mobile operation.

76 A "word" in International Morse code is defined as five alphabetic or numeric characters

77 At high code speeds, radio operators "hear" entire words, not individual letters, and they almost always are typing or writing the word or two they heard a fraction of a second before the word they currently are hearing. Ted's rusty Spanish forced him to copy most of the Fleet news broadcast character-by-character, something that can be excruciatingly tiring at high code speeds, even over a short period of time.

"You need to practice your Morse code, Teodoro," teased Marco at 3:30 AM one morning. "You never know when you may need it! If you were in the Chilean Navy under my command, I would have to demote you to Radioman Third Class until you got your code speed up! You would *never* earn enough money to return to your country!" There was no end of merriment in the shack, most at Ted's expense.

Ted thoroughly enjoyed these sessions in the ship's radio shack. Aside from the messages passed to the States, they had the added benefit of making the time at sea pass more quickly.

The ship's officers and visiting scientists had their dinners in the Captain's Mess, and frequently Ted was seated next to Lieutenant-Commander Cristian Barbudo, or 'Cristian', as he asked Ted to call him. Cristian, a deeply religious man, was just under six feet tall and physically trim, something he attributed to working out in the ship's gym every morning before breakfast. "It gives me a chance to clear my mind after going through my radio messages," he joked, when Ted asked how he found the time to stay in shape.

Cristian was four years older than Ted, married, and had two beautiful daughters, Daniela and Teresa. His wife, Maria, taught in a private school located near Viña del Mar, a major seaside resort town where they had made their home for the past four years.

Cristian loved to play chess, and the two men played several matches during the voyage, just to while away the hours.

"Come on, Teodoro, set up the board," the commander often would say, loud enough for everyone to hear. The officers of the *Piloto Pardo* loved to watch them battle it out, and more than a few Chilean escudos changed hands on bets that were placed at the start of each match.

It did not take long for Cristian and Ted to take each other's measure. From the very first game, each knew that his adversary was a worthy opponent, one who not only knew the game, but also, the latest moves and strategies.

"What are you grinning about, Teodoro?" asked the commander, who had won White, after they had completed their first six pairs of moves in the first game that afternoon.

"Well, sir, this looks like the opening of the second game between Mikhail Botvinnik and Mikhail Tal in 1960.[78] I don't know about you, but it won't be long before I'll have to play the rest of the game using my own skills. My memory isn't *that* good anymore."

Cristian laughed until tears were rolling down his cheeks. "I only can remember two or three of the openings from the 24 games in that match, Teodoro. Just my luck that you knew one of those games as well!"

Conversation during their games ranged far and wide, from Cristian's family, to his love of photography, to Ted's life as a graduate student in Madison. It appeared that Cristian was the ship's personnel officer. Ted had observed him entering and leaving the ship's radio shack frequently throughout the day and early evening hours. But then, given what Ted *thought* were his responsibilities, this would not have been unusual.

---

78 http://www.worldchesslinks.net/ezde1.html

However, Ted found a depth in their conversations, and particularly to Cristian's observations, that spoke to an intelligence far deeper than one associated simply with military matters. Cristian seemed, at times, more of a philosopher than one would have expected . . . someone bent on divining the motives of men as they went about their daily pursuits. Ted had the uneasy feeling that Cristian was looking deep into his soul while they played chess, even distracting him with disarming conversation while taking snapshots of his most hidden intentions and motives. *Maybe it is just his way of gaining insight into his opponent's psychological makeup. Yet*— Ted really was not sure what to make of what he was sensing.

"It's interesting, Teodoro," Cristian said early one morning around 2:00 AM as he studied the White *king* he was holding in front of him while they were putting the pieces away after a particularly complex game—one that he had won, though it was *not* without a struggle—"Chess really is nothing more than a metaphor for life itself. When the game is over, the *king* and the *pawn* both go into the same pine box.[79] It is our destiny, my friend."

By late on December 23rd, the Expedition was working its way south through the Tierra del Fuego Archipelago,[80] the southern-most point of which forms Cape Horn.[81]

No one on the voyage had to be an experienced seaman to know that the ship had crossed into the Drake Passage. Once

---

79 Italian proverb
80 http://www.ecophotoexplorers.com/antarctica_southocean.asp
81 http://en.wikipedia.org/wiki/Cape_Horn

through the Archipelago, the sea became increasing roiled, and the wind picked up dramatically. The convoy headed south, toward Deception Island in the South Shetland Islands, its intermediate destination. But first, it had to traverse that vast expanse of water between the tip of South America and the tip of the North Antarctic Peninsula, home to some of the most treacherous seas on Earth.

Depending on the latitude, sailors hear winds that *roar* (the *Roaring Forties*, from 40 to 50 degrees S. latitude), are *furious* (the *Furious Fifties*, from 50 to 60 degrees S. latitude), or literally *shriek* (the *Shrieking Sixties*, from 60 to 70 degrees S. latitude).[82] [83] [84]

"I hope you have your sea legs, Señor Stone!" It was the captain of the *Piloto Pardo*, Señor Ignacio Núñez Ballesteros. Ted was on the bridge at his invitation. "With no land masses to impede the winds," he explained, "waves on these waters can reach heights of seventy feet and more."[85] The captain's English was impeccable.

---

82 http://www.youtube.com/watch?v=Jld5pIUKhCE Storm on the Drake Passage. Note how some of the waves not only reach, but cover the windows of the ship. If you listen carefully, you can hear the sounds of objects being thrown about the cabin (and broken?). For waves to reach the windows of the bridge is a scary thought, indeed (worse if you ever experienced it!).

83 http://www.youtube.com/watch?v=ISQGTChuRyY&feature=related This is a film taken aboard the Antarctic Dream in Beaufort Force 12 winds (more than 73 miles per hour and wave heights greater than 46 feet) as it crossed the Drake Passage.

84 http://www.youtube.com/watch?v=S4PNjGjZijs&feature=related Passenger rescue operation at Point Wild, Antarctica. Watch how quickly a storm descends upon this ship, its Zodiacs, and their passengers in the waters off the South Shetland Islands.

85 Frank Worsley and Ernest Shackleton reported that the wave that engulfed the *James Caird* in the Drake Passage was 100 feet high. See http://www.pbs.org/wgbh/nova/shackletonexped/mail/mail19991029.html

"In addition to the wind and waves," he continued, "we are going to face an increasing array of water-borne ice from melting and calving of the Continental Glacier caused by heating during the austral summer. This ice will include sea-ice, iceberg fragments, small icebergs, and even huge icebergs hundreds or even thousands of yards across. Some will be much larger than the *Pardo*, I am sad to say! Of course, 90% of all floating ice *is below the surface*. Even ships specifically built for work in these waters have succumbed to the wind, waves, and ice."

Ted knew that, given the remoteness of the region, rescue may not always come in time to save a ship or its people.[86] [87] Adding to the danger was the fact that the life expectancy of an unprotected person in the water is measured in minutes.

As the flotilla continued south, the barometer dropped precipitously, signaling the impending arrival of a major storm. The wind rapidly increased to seventy-five miles per hour and so, too, did the height of the waves, some exceeding fifty feet. The three ships now were feeling the brunt of the storm, a full blown hurricane with Beaufort Force 12 winds.[88]

Professor O'Mhaille and Grant Morris were so seasick that the only thing David and Ted could do to make them comfortable was to strap them into two lower bunks. Large cooking pots with a little water at the bottom of each were tethered to the professor's and Morris's bunk frames for their use in the event

---

86 http://www.youtube.com/watch?v=a1cDBsLZNAg Antarctic cruise ship hits an iceberg and sinks.

87 http://www.mnn.com/transportation/planes-trains-bikes/stories/nz-wants-action-to-prevent-antarctic-cruise-disaster Grounding of the liner Ocean Nova was the fourth accident involving a passenger ship in Antarctica in just over a year.

88 http://www.stormfax.com/beaufort.htm

they became violently ill. There was no way either man could make his way to a railing, much less stand.

By now, anything neither tied nor bolted down in some fashion had been thrown against the bulkheads or hull. The Officer's Mess was a shambles, with food, furniture, broken plates, and eating utensils strewn everywhere. The cook managed to produce biscuits daily, but that was the only food available. When David and Ted felt hungry, they would make their way to the mess, stuff a few biscuits in their pockets, and head back to their bunks to read. The naval officers devised a game to see how long a person could stand on the deck in the Officer's Mess. "Come on, Teodoro!" yelled Lieutenant Alvarez above the roar of the hurricane. "Try your luck!" Ted lasted only ten seconds before he was thrown into the bulkhead. Ted saw men on the bridge strapping themselves into their chairs so that they could perform their duties.

Ted had been reading James A Mitchner's[89] *Hawaii* as a way to pass the time when he looked up at the chain hanging from a hook on the wall in their cabin. On it was a crucifix, which was swinging through a sixty degree arc, thirty degrees to one side, then thirty degrees to the other. *I'll take all the help I can get at this point,* he thought.

Actually, the Roman Catholic Church had danced in and out of his life since he was born in St. Agnes Hospital, Fond du Lac, WI, late in 1938. His family only spent a few years there before moving to Sheboygan during World War II, where his father worked in a munitions factory. After the war, by which time the

89 http://www.achievement.org/autodoc/page/micobio-1

family had moved to Milwaukee, an uncle, who had decided to move to Florida permanently, gave Solly, Ted's dad, his home north of Fond du Lac on the shores of Lake Winnebago. So, beginning in the early 1950s, when Ted still was in high school, the family returned to Fond du Lac every summer, where Ted worked at the Lake Park Outdoor Theater.

Because his 'day' began around 6:00 PM and lasted well into the early hours of the next morning, Ted almost always took an hour nap around 4:00 PM. Donning a set of headphones plugged into a small transistor radio he had built, he never failed to fall into a deep sleep.

It so happened that at 4:00 PM every day of the week, the Holy Family Catholic Community of Fond du Lac sponsored an hour-long broadcast on KFIZ-AM, the 250-Watt radio station located just across the lake from the Stone summer home. It was the only station that Ted could receive consistently on his transistor radio. Day after day he was treated to discussions of and quotes from the New Testament, as well as the saying of the Rosary. All of this material filtered into his subconscious in a process akin to *osmosis* so that, eventually, he knew a fair amount about the Church and its liturgy *without even being aware of having acquired this knowledge.*

Ted closed his eyes and thought about those carefree summer days and wonderful nights, distant memories never to be enjoyed again. The irony did not escape him of his having been raised—at least in part—in a heavily Roman Catholic part of the country, and now, working with deeply religious people of the same faith half a world away. He smiled, thinking that his best friend on the Expedition, Lieutenant-Commander Jorge Barbudo, was a devout Catholic, though the subject of religion had *never* come up in their conversations. *I guess there are some things that good friends just silently accept and having done so, move on.*

And then, without warning, a monstrous wave struck the ship on the starboard side. It was a huge *rogue*. The helmsman later said it must have been sixty feet high, given the amount of water that reached the bridge's windows. It hit the ship broadside, sending it careening to port and momentarily interrupting the ship's electrical system.

In the flickering light following the impact, Ted saw the crucifix swing sharply to port, traversing an arc of more than forty degrees. Somewhere close to his cabin a heavy object, perhaps a chair that had not been secured firmly against the hull, hit a bulkhead with a resounding *crash*. He heard sounds of its splintered remnants clattering across the steel deck and echoing down the passageway.

It took several seconds before the ship recovered its equilibrium, only to swing an equal amount to starboard as the storm raged unabated. The electrical system recovered. But with the temperature in the cabin hovering around 45 degrees and the hurricane intensifying, Ted's life, and the lives of everyone on the Expedition, hung in the balance.

Reaching land, *any land*, now dominated Ted's every thought.

Christmas came and went. Because of the hurricane, the officers and men could not join together for a celebration. In fact, everyone who was not absolutely essential to the operation and safety of the ship stayed in his bunk.

When he was not reading *Hawaii*, Ted read old issues of *QST* and *CQ*, magazines devoted to ham radio, which he had brought with him. *If I still lived at home and was going to high school,* he thought, *I'd probably be building one project or another from among those described in these magazines for my station. I'd also be taking time out to meet Father John Haas, W9UJF (SK),*[90] *of Queen of Apostles Seminary in Madison, WI, on the air for our daily schedule.*

Father Haas was an old friend with whom he had kept a daily schedule at 4:30 PM local time on the 80-meter Amateur band throughout his high school years. Their communications using the International Morse code were designed to assist the Seminary and St. Anthony's in Milwaukee in coordinating their mutual activities. So, for more than three years, Ted and Father Haas met daily to exchange messages such as: *To the St. Anthony's House Keeper: Fr. Joe just left for home.*

When he was in Milwaukee, Fr. Haas never missed an opportunity to drop by for some of Ted's mother's cooking. "Myrtle, you make the best matzoh ball soup I've ever tasted. You know, I can't get food like this in the Seminary!" The good Father was always invited to the Stone home around the winter holidays, when Myrtle presented him a tin full of her special cheese cookies and powdered donuts,[91] treats that year

---

90 Fr. John Haas was a Pallottine priest who has long since passed away. Queen of Apostles closed in 1979, and the building was torn down in 2002. (Source: Ms. Mary C. Uhler, Editor, Catholic Herald Newspaper, Madison, WI, personal communication, March 24, 2010.) When an amateur radio operator passes away, his code key is said to have gone silent, and so, he or she is referred to as a silent key, with (SK) appended to their call sign.

91 Famed donuts of the Salvation Army, from a recipe developed during World War I

after year Father Haas devoured before he even returned to Madison.

Discussions at the dinner table during the Father's visits invariably turned to the Old and New Testaments, and to comparing and contrasting the two Bibles and their messages. The conversations, mostly between Ted's father Solly and Father Haas, never failed to enlighten Ted in matters religious. They certainly expanded his knowledge of the Roman Catholic faith far beyond what he might otherwise have acquired in his day-to-day comings and goings. Fr. Haas also looked forward to discussing many aspects of Judaism with the Stones, including *Prophets,*[92] which always had intrigued him and on which Solly was an expert. Fr. Haas sometimes compared their many conversations over dinner to the advanced courses he took in comparative religion.

Those were great days, Ted thought, as the swinging crucifix on the wall lulled him to sleep.

When he woke on the morning of December 26th, the storm was abating, though it still represented a considerable threat to the flotilla. At the peak of the storm, winds exceeded eighty miles per hour according to the meteorologist onboard; gusts reached 100 miles per hour.

On his way to the Officer's Mess, Ted encountered the captain of the *Piloto Pardo* in a passageway. The man, still smartly dressed in his neatly pressed uniform but looking exhausted, took off his wire rim glasses and gently rubbed his eyes with his thumb and forefinger. Shaking his head from side

---

92 See, for example, The Prophets: A New Translation Of The Holy Scriptures According To The Traditional Hebrew Text, The Jewish Publication Society of America, Philadelphia, Pennsylvania, 1978

to side, he lamented, "I have participated in seven expeditions to the Antarctic. I have talked with my predecessors by radio. This one was by far the worst crossing in the history of Chilean Antarctic Expeditions!"

By the morning of December 27th, the ships were standing off the entrance to the harbor at Deception Island in the South Shetland Islands. They had crossed the Drake Passage and were safe. Except for minor damage to all three ships—damage that already was being repaired by the ships' crews—the Expedition was proceeding on schedule. Now it was time for Ted to tie the South American Gravity Network to the soon-to-be-established Chilean Antarctic Gravity Network by first linking Punta Arenas to British Base B on Deception Island.

The operational pace was picking up.

VII
Nature's Deception

Approached from the north, Deception Island gives the appearance of being a solid land mass, no different from any other island found in the world's oceans. In fact, the island, near the southern end of the South Shetland Islands, is one of Antarctica's two *active* volcanoes.[93] The center of the island comprises a four-mile-wide caldera flooded with sea water.[94] In Nature, as in Man, the potential to deceive is always present.

The only way into the harbor is through a narrow passage on the southeast side of the island known as Neptune's Bellows. A wrecked ship on the rocks at the mouth of the harbor serves as a warning to all seamen. Rocks near the surface to one side of the entrance add to the danger. However, a good navigator can bring his ship through the Bellows safely.

---

93 Mr. Erebus is the other active volcano in Antarctica

94 http://www.deceptionisland.aq/

The only way into the harbor is through a narrow passage on the southeast side of the island known as Neptune's Bellows.[95]

Until the mid-to-late 1960s, the island provided one of the safest harbors in the Antarctic—Port Foster.[96] In the early 1960s, the rim of the caldera was home to three scientific research bases: Chilean Base Pedro Aguirre Cerda (PAC), British Base B, and Argentine Base Deception. While the island has been claimed by Chile, the United Kingdom, and Argentina, it falls under the jurisdiction of the Antarctic Treaty System.[97] Maps of, and postage stamps from, Chile and Argentina in the 1960s showed they included the North Antarctic Peninsula as their national territory. No love was lost between the Chilean and Argentine military personnel on Deception Island.

95 Photo by author

96 Volcanic eruptions in 1967 and 1969 caused serious damage to the three scientific stations along the rim of the caldera. The only current research bases on the island are run by the Argentine Army and Spain. See: http://en.wikipedia.org/wiki/Deception_Island

97 http://www.eoearth.org/article/Antarctic_Treaty_System

The ships of the 16th Chilean Expedition approached Deception Island from the north early on December 27, 1961. Moving around the eastern side of the island, they passed Bailey Head,[98] a high ridge produced by ancient lava flows adjacent to a black gravel beach of ground volcanic rocks. The rookery here is one of the largest found anywhere in the Antarctic. More than 100,000 Chinstrap penguins[99] [100] make Deception Island their home.

Ted long had hoped he would get a glimpse of the colony, if even from afar. The nearby beach and surrounding area was criss-crossed with well-worn paths that had been beaten into the basaltic sand and rock over time by the feet of hundreds of thousands of penguins making their way to and from the ocean searching for food and small stones. The latter are used to build their nests. Here and there Ted could see a lone penguin stealing a stone surreptitiously from an unattended neighbor's nest, thereby saving the thief a trip to the sea and avoiding the risk posed by the leopard seals and orcas that frequented the waters to the east of the rookery. In one sense, then, such actions were a matter of survival.

Hundreds of penguins could be seen entering and exiting the water at any given time, reminding Ted of a small city and the movement of people and their cars—up and down sidewalks and roads. It was a sight he would never forget.

The sea was calm. As the ships lined up to enter the harbor, the captain of the *Piloto Pardo* ordered one of the ship's two

---

98 http://drandmrsrock.com/antarctica_bailey.html

99 http://www.animalsandearth.com/view/42770

100 http://www.cuboimages.it/preview.asp?filename=SES0164.jpg&s=&cs=&csnot=&sortType=0&ls=&s1=&s2=&s3=&op1=&op2=&photographerCode=SES&country=&rights=&archiveID=&p=26

helicopters to fly to the British Base on the island. Aboard the little Bell two-seat helicopter with the familiar goldfish-bowl canopy were the pilot and Ted, and Worden #14.

The sole purpose for Ted being aboard was to tie the harbor gravity station in Punta Arenas to the gravity station at British Base B, a site on the Antarctic Gravity Network. This would provide the drift information needed on the gravimeter for future data-reduction purposes. The readings taken at British Base B also would form the basis for the new gravity network to be established among the Chilean Antarctic stations in the South Shetland Islands as well as on the North Antarctica Peninsula.

The helicopter set down on the base's airfield and was met by the base radio operator, a jovial young man who introduced himself as 'Front'. "Hi, mate," he shouted as Ted stepped out of the helicopter and, ducking his head, walked toward him. "Welcome to Base B. We haven't had so much excitement since the summer contingent left for the U.K. last March! It's great to see some new faces!"

Ted could not help noticing that the front of his sweatshirt read 'Front to Front' while the back read 'Back to Front'. *I guess wintering over in the Antarctic can do strange things to your mind.*

"So, what brings you to our base?" asked Front. "I thought you would have flown first to the Chilean Air Force base."

Ted explained that he needed to use his gravimeter to tie the station in Punta Arenas into the Antarctic Gravity Network by occupying British Base B's gravity site. "I will visit the gravity site at the Chilean base later this morning when the Expedition's ships sail into the harbor. But when the opportunity arose to fly into the British Base, I thought it would make a good chance to acquire some gravity data there before my schedule gets complicated. All I need to do now is find the base's gravity site."

"And where might that be?" asked Front in his clipped British accent.

"Well," said Ted, "according to my records, the gravity site is located in the boat house. There should be a British Antarctic Survey (BAS) plate on the floor in the boat house. That's where I need to take the readings."

They soon found the BAS plate, and within twenty minutes, Ted had the gravimeter readings he needed. With that, he thanked Front and returned to the helicopter for the flight back to the *Piloto Pardo.*

By now, the three ships were moving into Port Foster, the completely enclosed harbor within the caldera, to offload both personnel and cargo at Chilean Base PAC.

After returning to the *Piloto Pardo,* Ted ran into Commander Barbudo. "I'm being transferred to the *Lientur* for the remainder of the Expedition, Teodoro. They have assigned me the position of Executive Officer.

"Unfortunately, the man who now holds that position must return to Chile on the first vessel returning to Punta Arenas . . . something about a family emergency," continued Cristian. "So, I'll move over and take his place. We'll still see one another, my friend. I would hope, too, that we'll have an opportunity to play an occasional game of chess during those times when the *Lientur* is called upon to support your field efforts."

They shook hands, gave each other *un abrazo*[101] while patting one another on the back, and waved good-bye. There was no way of knowing when they would see each other again.

With the three ships anchored together in Port Foster, it was easy for Ted to transfer to a launch for a visit to Base PAC. There, he occupied a gravity site at the base of the flagpole in the front of the base's main building.

With the ships' crews still transporting material to shore after he had finished taking his gravity readings, Ted took a few minutes to walk down to the beach and survey the landscape. The water was steaming, and it felt warm to the touch. This was not unexpected; after all, the island was a volcano. Much of the island was snow-covered, and the only flora were moss and lichen. There were, reportedly, nine species of seabird on the island, though few were seen in the interior. Similarly, while the largest colony of penguins was located on the southeast coast, Ted saw none in the warm harbor waters. Taken together, the island was a unique habitat.

As he walked along the deserted beach, he thought about some of the interesting people whom he had met on his way south . . . the breadth of their humanity . . . the simple pleasure that came from knowing them. There were, of course, Professors James Trimble and Michael Granger at the University of Miami, Professor Victor Martinez, of the University of Peru's Department of Geology, and Professor Alejandro Barría, one of the most renowned geologists and seismologists in North and South America. And who could forget Señor Joaquín Covas? Without him, Punta Arenas would have been a bore,

---

101 The phrase simply means a strong hug (equivalent to a "bear hug")

though U.S. Air Force Captain Frank Lawson certainly made life interesting by pinning his ears back in chess!

And then there is his good friend, Lieutenant-Commander Cristian Barbudo, another chess player who has been giving him a run for his money. And what an honor it has been to meet and work with such fine naval officers as Capitán Roberto Muñoz of the *Lientur* and the captain of the *Piloto Pardo*, Señor Ignacio Núñez Ballesteros. The richness he found in these relationships was beyond his wildest expectations.

"And?" demanded Bellolio, the instant Lucero stepped over the railing of the *Lientur* after climbing the rope ladder from the motor launch.

"Be quiet!" hissed Lucero, grabbing Bellolio's arm and pulling him to the port side of the ship.

"Well, what did you find?"

"The crate came through the storm without a scratch," whispered Lucero. "Remember, *I* was the one who put it in the hold. I put it in a corner, against a bulkhead and the hull. It was strapped down tight and wedged behind other crates as well. There was *no way* it could have moved unless the ship broke up, God forbid!

"Now, mind you, I have no idea what the *inside* of that refrigerator looks like. With all that gold clanking around in there, it probably took a real beating. But who cares? Once we take our loot and pay off Leonardo, he can tell his wife the refrigerator was damaged in a stormy crossing, and he will apply to the Navy for a replacement. He won't be the only one, I'll tell you that. You should have seen the mess in the *Piloto*

Pardo's hold. At least five crates broke loose. There was parts of refrigerators and stoves all over the place. I don't know about you, Eduardo, but that was the worst storm I have *ever* been through at sea!"

By mid-afternoon, final preparations were underway for the movement of personnel and supplies to Base O'Higgins. Unfortunately, in coming down some stairs on the *Piloto Pardo* following lunch, Professor O'Mhaille slipped and fell, severely reinjuring his back. The ship's doctor told him that under no circumstances could he exert himself. In fact, he told the professor it would be best if he returned home to the United States on the first ship back to Chile. O'Mhaille, in agonizing pain, knew that returning home was his only option. In the meantime, he would stay on the *Piloto Pardo* until a ship returned to Chile for purposes of rotating personnel and bringing additional supplies down for the coming winter.

O'Mhaille, totally disheartened and furious with himself over his accident, told his two graduate students what he expected of them. "We've planned this trip and the field work carefully. We have the areas mapped, and we know what we're looking for. Grant, you have Ted to help you gather, bag, and mark samples. David, you know what needs to be done when you arrive at Base GGV. Refine your maps and gather as many samples as is physically possible. We'll sort it all out when we get back to Madison. I have nothing but the fullest confidence in you and your capabilities."

Late in the afternoon on December 27th, the *Yelcho* weighed anchor and set a course to the northeast for Base Arturo Prat on Greenwich Island. The *Piloto Pardo* and the *Lientur* set a course to the east for Base O'Higgins, about eighteen miles southwest of the most northerly point of the North Antarctic Peninsula. O'Higgins is situated just above the Antarctic Circle at 63°19′15″S, 57°53′55″W. It is at a latitude known as the 'Banana Belt' among Antarctic researchers who work in the colder climes much farther south, and especially by those who work at the South Pole.

Ted was not fooled. He had heard stories of the weather in the Banana Belt and especially of the weather over the Bransfield Strait, a 60-mile wide body of water laden with icebergs and other forms of floating ice that lies between the South Shetland Islands and North Antarctic Peninsula. There was no question in *anyone's* mind that the Bransfield was among the most dangerous bodies of water in the world.[102]

Fortunately, the Expedition's crossing proceeded without incident, and the two ships arrived at Base O'Higgins early in the morning on December 28th. With the ocean bottom too smooth to anchor and icebergs in the area, both ships maintained power and continually maneuvered to avoid collisions with the ice. Unloading would begin the next day; now it was time for a celebration. The 16th Chilean Expedition to the Antarctic had arrived at Base O'Higgins for the austral summer!

Unloading of the cargo from the *Piloto Pardo* and the *Lientur* began immediately upon arrival. Their cargos, including

---

102 On November 23, 2007, the MS Explorer struck an iceberg and sank in the Bransfield Strait. See: http://en.wikipedia.org/wiki/MS_Explorer

crates and other large containers, were transferred from the ships to the dock using motor launches. Once on land, cargo was taken up the hill to the base on a flatbed cart pulled by a small tractor. CWO Lucero took an uncommon interest in the unloading of the *Piloto Pardo*, given his regular duties on the *Lientur*. But then, no one thought anything of it because of the spirit of camaraderie that prevailed among the Army and Navy personnel at all levels.

VIII
Base General Bernardo O'Higgins Riquelme

Base Bernardo O'Higgins, a wind- and snow-swept outpost on the North Antarctic Peninsula, is one of the oldest, permanent bases on the Frozen Continent, having been in continuous operation since February 18, 1948.[103] [104] Operated by the Chilean Army, it is located on a small peninsula that juts out from the North Antarctic Peninsula. Seen from the mountain to the south, the base had all the appearance of a small, abandoned mining town on a planet at the outer reaches of the galaxy.

---

103 See, for example, http://en.wikipedia.org/wiki/Base_General_Bernardo_O'Higgins_Riquelme

104 For another photograph of Base O'Higgins, see http://www.antarktis-station.de/. The photograph at the top of the Web page was taken from a mountain that is located to the south of the base, the same position from which the photograph above was taken by the author.

Base Bernardo O'Higgins: Seen from the mountain to the south, the base had all the appearance of a small, abandoned mining town on a planet at the outer reaches of the galaxy.[105]

In late 1961, the base consisted of one large building that housed personnel living quarters, a living room, offices, a kitchen, storage rooms, and two radio shacks, one for the military, and one for Amateur use, the latter having the call sign CE9AF. Ted saw that one room off to the right side of the base housed twin, 40-kW diesel generators that supplied electricity to the base. *Well, I'll be!* he chuckled to himself when he saw them for the first time. "Look, Grant," he yelled as Morris passed by the room, "these generators were manufactured in South Milwaukee, eight miles from where my folks live!"

One generator was pressed into service every evening from 5:00 PM to 11:00 PM, its steady *hum* a comfort to all in the base. No base-wide electricity was available during the day, though smaller generators were available to support military communications, welding operations, and other critical needs

105 Photo by author

during work hours. The second generator was maintained on standby status, should the primary unit fail.

Behind the kitchen was a room dedicated to water production. It contained a large stainless steel drum heated by a fuel oil burner, with piping that led to a sealed reservoir. An electric pump was used to distribute water to the kitchen and bathroom, both of which were located adjacent to the room in which the fresh water was produced. A 200-gallon water heater, also heated by a fuel oil burner, maintained a ready supply of hot water for cooking, sanitary, and bathing purposes.

In all, the base could accommodate eighteen men, three times the number that had wintered-over. Still, once the Expedition's ships left the area, those who stayed behind faced a lonely existence. No tourist ships stopped at O'Higgins. So, except for the infrequent return of a Chilean naval vessel during the summer, the only other way that visitors might arrive would by dogsled . . . and such visits were a remote possibility at best.

Teams of enlisted men, rotated throughout the month on a schedule set by the base commandant, were responsible for ensuring the ready availability of ice at the melting facility. Ted knew that there was a technique for making fresh water by freezing sea water.[106] However, it was far easier for the men at O'Higgins to use small icebergs as a source of the base's fresh-water supply. These icebergs, which had calved from the

---

106 Freezing salt water will indeed turn it into fresh water. It takes several years for the process to make the sea-ice salt-free enough for people to melt and use it for drinking water, but they can and have done this for centuries. The Book of Popular Science, Grolier Incorporated, New York, NY, 1967; http://www.madsci.org/posts/archives/2001-02/982120143.Es.r.html

Continental Glacier and had floated near the base's dock, were broken into small chunks several cubic feet in size using picks. Then, they were loaded on the flatbed cart for transport to the base. Here, they were unloaded, stored next to the door of the melting room, and brought in as needed throughout the day.

The dog kennel was located 100 feet behind the base. Home to twelve dogs of various sizes and breeds—seven that had wintered over and five that were brought down by members of the current Expedition—its inhabitants were and would continue to be a constant source of noise that could be heard by anyone who stepped outside. There simply was no way to stop the constant dog fights that occurred among the animals.

It was intended that the dogs pull sleds the Chilean Army would employ on its explorations of the Antarctic Peninsula. Ted knew from his readings that BAS research teams had used this form of transportation for decades with great success.

Chilean Army First Sergeant Fernando Quesada was responsible for feeding the dogs. He would be wintering-over, and for any number of reasons, was not happy. His face bore a permanent mask of dissatisfaction.

"To reduce the amount of refrigerated freight brought to the Antarctica by the Expedition to the absolute minimum," he told Ted as they talked several hours after the Expedition arrived, "little dog food was shipped south from Punta Arenas. In fact, there only was enough for the voyage and the first two weeks following the arrival of the ships at O'Higgins. It will be my responsibility to provide food for the dogs for the rest of the year. By all estimates, we will have to kill roughly 180 seals during the summer season if we are to have enough dog food to last through the winter and until the ships return next December. Let me show you around the area."

The base had two front entrances, both at ground level. Above the entrance on the left was a small room that housed a meteorological observatory. The instruments monitored there were fastened to ground-mounted masts erected on either side of the door. The entrance to the right had what appeared to be a second entrance to a small room built on the second level. This second-story 'entrance', however, could only be accessed using a stairway inside the base. "That door," said the sergeant, "allows wintering-over parties to leave the building when wind-driven snow reaches heights that block the first floor exits."

A wide variety of wire antennas criss-crossed the structure overhead at heights ranging from thirty to fifty feet. They provided the military and Amateur radio stations with access to all frequencies in the medium and high-frequency bands.

Ted assumed that earlier in the year, in March, 1961 to be exact, just before the last ship departed for Chile and the personnel wintering over hunkered down for the long austral winter, the building had received a coat of bright orange paint. Now, in the harsh light of day—a day that lasted close to twenty-three hours—the base he was looking at appeared dull in color. It had been 'sanded' down to the wood by winter wind-driven ice pellets and snow that at times impacted the structure at speeds of up to 150 miles per hour while the temperature outside was -40 degrees Fahrenheit.[107] Under these conditions, it would not

---

107 Wind chills only are computed for winds under 110 miles per hour. For winds of 109 miles per hour and a winter temperature of -40 degrees Fahrenheit, which is not unusual for Base O'Higgins during the austral winter, the wind chill is -101 degrees Fahrenheit. http://www.nws.noaa.gov/os/windchill/index.shtml

have been possible for the men to leave the base for any reason but one—a major fire.

A second building, located some distance from the first, was vacant, but stocked and ready for occupancy in the event the main structure burned down. "That actually occurred during the 1958 International Geophysical Year, the IGY," said Sergeant Quesada, snuffing out his cigarette on a rock. "The main base burned to the ground."

Well, that's comforting, thought Ted, watching burning ashes from the sergeant's cigarette butt fly toward the base in the wind coming off the Bransfield Strait. He left the sergeant to tend to his dogs and headed to where the University's luggage and equipment had been placed. Grabbing his duffle bag, he entered the main base and made his way to the room to which he and Grant had been assigned. It was a small room to the left side of the base. Ted saw that it had a small window, perhaps one-foot-square, that gave them a view to the southwest, across the small rock-strewn peninsula on which the base had been built, to the Bransfield Strait.

The entire base was eternally cold. Daytime room temperatures hovered in the mid-40s. This was not surprising, given that outside temperatures were generally in the range of thirty to fifty degrees at this time of year and that no heat was provided during the day.

Ted's first order of business, performed immediately upon landing at the base, was to establish a new gravity station and tie that station into the Antarctic Gravity Network by taking a set of readings with the gravimeter. The site chosen was at the base of a concrete platform upon which rested the bust of O'Higgins. "David, would you take some readings as well, just to refresh your memory on its operation and the data to be collected?" Ted called out as David came up the hill from the pier, where unloading operations were continuing at a feverish pace. The *Lientur* was scheduled to leave that night for Base Gabriel González Videla (GGV), some two degrees south in latitude. David would be onboard, and the gravimeter would go with him.

With the data acquired, the men repacked the gravimeter in its canister. "It's all yours, David. I understand that the Chileans have a science building at GGV and may even have made preparations to determine the pull of gravity there by building a pendulum station. Perhaps you could establish a gravimetry site in the same location." David nodded.

"One more thing. The Chileans have a base called Sub-Base Yelcho on Anvers Island, to the south of Base GGV. The captain of the *Piloto Pardo* mentioned that there is a heliport on that base. If you get down there, the heliport's concrete pad might make a good place to establish a gravimetry site."

David smiled. "I see how deftly you got this monkey off your back, sir! Just make sure Dr. Woollard knows how much work your brilliant colleague who is majoring in geology did for the science of geophysics!"

Ted had no choice. His job was to stay at Base O'Higgins and support Grant's mapping and sample collection efforts. If all went well, he would link up with David sometime in January or early February in the South Shetland Islands. Then, he would again assume responsibility for the gravimeter.

The *Lientur*, with David onboard, would stay at Base O'Higgins through New Years Day before leaving for Base GGV. Once he left, it would be February before David and Ted would see each other again.

The *Piloto Pardo* stayed at Base O'Higgins through New Years Day before moving down the Antarctic Peninsula. The purpose of its voyage would be to make official stops at bases maintained by the United States and Great Britain. In the third week of January, it was scheduled to rendezvous at Deception Island with the *Lautaro,*[108] another Chilean Antarctic rescue tug supporting the Expedition by bringing supplies and mail from South America. At that time, Professor O'Mhaille would transfer to the *Lautaro* for the trip back to South America on his return to the United States.

While everyone waited for the New Year, the crews of both ships helped the Army detachment at O'Higgins refurbish the base as well as repair the damage wrought by the past winter's onslaught. There were new radio masts and antennas to be erected, and the base needed a new coat of orange paint as well. But with continuous daylight, the work proceeded around the clock. There was no question that when the time came for the Navy to leave, the base would be 'ship-shape'.

A low level of heat was provided during the times that people slept, when the outside temperatures fell as the sun dropped in the sky and dipped briefly under the horizon. But the heat served only to drive the relative humidity down to levels into the single digits, which made everyone uncomfortable.

[108] http://www.navsource.org/archives/09/38/38122.htm

Ted waited until the heat and electricity were brought up his first night at the base, then took a shower, the first since leaving Punta Arenas. Toweling dry, he put on a fresh set of insulated underwear, climbed into his sleeping bag, which was lying on the lower bunk, donned his dark eye shades—the sun still was high in the sky—and fell fast asleep. It was a little after 11:00 PM.

He awoke at 5:00 AM, unable to speak. The air was so dry that his mouth and throat were totally parched. *This is just great,* he thought. *If I stay inside the base, I won't be able to talk the entire time I'm here!*

After he got dressed, he walked outside and uncrated one of the two-man tents that the team had brought with them from Madison for use in their field work at Base O'Higgins. After breakfast, he erected it next to the fuel dump using two long cast-iron pipes to tie off the tent ropes. Grant came out and saw what he was doing. "That's a great idea," he crackled, his voice barely audible. Two minutes later he returned with both of their sleeping bags. From that point on, if the two men were at Base O'Higgins, as opposed to being in the field or on a ship, they slept in that tent, and they did so up to the day they left the base for home.

The festivities on New Year's Eve, December 31, 1961 did not begin until an hour before midnight, though the sun still was high in the sky. They began with everyone drinking a milk-coffee mixture and telling jokes. At the stroke of midnight, everyone gave one another *un abrazo* and shook hands. Private First Class Rámon Escobar, who stood two feet shorter than

Ted, brought out a box to be tall enough to put his hands around Ted for *un abrazo,* the only way to really ring in the New Year properly with close friends!

It was 1:00 AM when everyone sat down to dinner. The table was covered with plates of chicken, potato salad, crackers, eggs, cookies, and cake, and, of course, pitchers of red and white wine. By 2:00 AM, everyone was telling jokes and singing, which only got louder with time, and by 3:00 AM, some of the men were dancing. It was not until 4:15 AM that Ted felt his head starting to spin, and when he went outside for some fresh air, the sun already was up. He never made it back to the party, choosing instead to seek the comfort of his tent and sleeping bag, where he slept soundly until 1:00 PM that afternoon.

It was the most unusual New Year's celebration he *ever* would experience!

IX
Unbridled Greed, Horrific Consequences

With the *Lientur* docked at O'Higgins, it only was a matter of time before Lucero and Bellolio sought out Rodríguez. No one thought it unusual that the Navy and Army non-commissioned officers were talking to one another. This was a wonderful opportunity for members of these two services to exchange souvenirs, 'war stories', and, in general, just enjoy some time together after unloading the ship's cargo that had been destined for the Army base.

For Lucero and Rodríguez, it was a time to relax and renew old acquaintances, to talk about their days in school together decades earlier, Rodríguez's family, and their careers in the two Chilean military services. It also was time for Lucero to introduce Bellolio and to let Rodríguez in on their plan.

Rodríguez already knew about the refrigerator that Lucero ostensibly had purchased for him. It was, after all, stored in the main building at Base O'Higgins. Now it was time to let him in on the fact that, for better or for worse, he was part of something that involved the theft of millions of dollars of cash, negotiable securities, gold coins, and jewelry stolen from the Banco Central de Chile in Talcahuano . . . spoils that were stored in *his* refrigerator . . . the one to be delivered to his home in Arica in March at the end of the Expedition.

"We need to talk to you, private like," said Lucero to Rodríguez, after introducing Bellolio to his old friend. The three men slipped away from the base and walked down the hill to the north, beyond the dog kennel. "Something important has come up that could, if things go well, bring a lot of money your way at the end of the Expedition."

Rodríguez's interest was piqued. But it was already late in the work day, and dinner soon would be served. Besides, Lucero and Bellolio were needed back on the *Lientur* that evening, so whatever they needed to talk about would have to wait until the following day.

Rodríguez had a thought. "I'm supposed to lead a seal hunting party tomorrow morning. Instead of taking two Army enlisted men, I'll explain to my captain that I'm taking two Navy non-coms, just to give them a new experience. Your job is to convince your superior officer to let you use a motorized launch from your ship for the hunting party."

Lucero and Bellolio secured the necessary permission from their superior officer, as did Rodríguez from the base commandant, *with the proviso that the seal hunt not last more than four hours*. There was much work to be done on the base as well as aboard the two ships, and they were needed to supervise.

Early the next morning, Lucero and Bellolio brought one of the *Lientur's* 21-foot-long motorized launches to the Base O'Higgins's dock. Lucero was serving as the motorman while Bellolio served as the helmsman. Rodríguez jumped in with two .32-caliber rifles, three hunting knives, and an assortment of nylon ropes. He took a seat in the bow.

The men set course for the northwest, toward a low, barren island barely visible in the dense fog that had enveloped the area during the early morning hours.

Ted stood at the top of a hill overlooking the channel between the base and the nearby islands. Something was wrong, but he could not put his finger on it. For one thing, little, if any, wildlife could be seen in the water. Normally, given his vantage point, he would have seen hundreds of penguins and seals moving about in the water or resting on the ice floating in front of him. But this morning, not one penguin or seal could be seen. *I wonder if this might be related to the incident I heard about yesterday?*

Just before noon that day, three Army enlisted men had taken a small motorized launch out to sea to hunt seals. When they returned, they described how, at one point, the waters near a large Gentoo[109] penguin rookery erupted in a frenzy of panic-stricken penguins, all of which obviously were attempting to exit the water at the same time. Some shot straight up into the air before swimming rapidly toward sanctuary, be it on land or on one of the many icebergs in the area.

Moments later, a pod of seven adult and three young orcas, also known as killer whales,[110] appeared. According to the Army enlisted men, the largest of the killer whales was about twenty feet long[111] and probably weighed several tons. One adult killer whale came within a foot of their launch, so close, in fact,

109 http://en.wikipedia.org/wiki/Gentoo_Penguin
110 http://en.wikipedia.org/wiki/Killer_Whale
111 7 meters is approximately 23 feet

that the men could have put their fists into the one-foot-wide blowhole on its head. The men described how they sat frozen in fear, how they dared not breathe. Fortunately, the orca soon lost interest in the launch and rejoined the pod.

When the pod was sufficiently distant from the launch to allow for escape, the men beat a hasty retreat to the base. By then, the *only* creatures they could see in the water were the killer whales. As far as they could see, the waters had been emptied of *all* penguins and seals. In the air, only a few skuas[112] circled.

Upon their return to Base O'Higgins, one man was treated for heart palpitations. All vowed that they never again would go out on the water in a small boat, orders from their superiors notwithstanding.

As Ted stood watching the launch disappear into the fog, the men carefully guiding it among pack ice and small icebergs, it finally dawned on him why he saw no sea life: *killer whales were in the area.*

Once Lucero, Bellolio, and Rodríguez were far enough from the base that they no longer could be seen, Lucero cut the engine. He motioned for Bellolio and Rodríguez to join him in the center of the boat.

"First," said Rodríguez, "thank you, Raul, from the bottom of my heart, for our new refrigerator. Life has not been easy on

---

[112] Skuas are fiercely predatory, and the species of the Southern Ocean are no exception. During the summer, South Polar skuas stake territories near Adélie penguin rookeries on the coast, raiding them for eggs, chicks, and also cleaning up carrion. Thus, they have earned the nickname, 'raptor of the south'. (From: http://www.antarcticconnection.com/antarctic/wildlife/birds/skuas.shtml)

Juanita, what with me gone most of the time and her having to take care of the three children. This will mean a lot to her, and coming from you, it means a lot to me. *Tu es un amigo bueno, y yo nunca me olvidaré su bondad.*"[113]

"Well, that is what we need to talk to you about."

Lucero quickly apprised Rodríguez as to what happened the previous May in Talcahuano, about the earthquake, how he and Bellolio were assigned to guard the bank, and what happened there.

"Look, Leonardo, Eduardo and I took a bunch of stuff out of the safe deposit boxes—cash, securities, gold coins, and jewelry—and we packed them in your new refrigerator, which we then recrated. We filled out all the paperwork in *your* name and had the crate shipped to the Fleet Warehouse in Punta Arenas so it could be loaded onto the *Piloto Pardo* for the voyage to Antarctica."

"You *what?* You did *what?*"

"Calm down, calm down, let me explain.

"The refrigerator is stored at Base O'Higgins. You've seen it. When the Expedition ends, it and the stuff will be shipped to your home in Arica, courtesy the Chilean Army. There, we'll open it, empty it, give you a fair share, plug in Juanita's new refrigerator, and scram. Eduardo and me plan to cross the Peruvian border and disappear. What you do with your share is up to you, as long as you sit on it for a year so that the *Carabiñeros* don't get wise to us!"

Rodríguez's eyes were bulging. "How could you do this to me? I have a wife and three children. If anything happens to me, what is going to happen to them? The Army will take

113 "You are a good friend, and I never will forget your kindness."

away my pension and throw me in prison. How will my family live?

"Look, I know I've done some pretty rotten things in my life, and I'm not proud of it! But after those two problems in Antofagasta four years ago, I put my life straight and finally regained my former pay grade. Now what the hell am I supposed to do?

"And just what do you mean by giving me my fair share? What the hell is that supposed to mean?" Rodríguez, gesturing wildly with his hands, was becoming more agitated by the minute.

Lucero put up his left hand, trying to calm Rodríguez. "Take it easy, Leonardo. We're giving you $1 million bucks. That's more money than you'll ever see in your entire life. What are you going to do? Stay in the Army forever? How much can you make doing that? Besides, our country's money isn't worth the paper it's printed on![114] This is your one chance to take care of your family. Take the cash. You won't have to worry about hiding the gold, getting rid of the securities, fencing the jewelry, or any of the other problems Eduardo and me will have."

Rodríguez tried to get his head around the number. "A million bucks, huh? U.S. money?" He could not even comprehend what $1 million looked like.

"I don't know, Raul, it's awful risky. I don't want to spend the rest of my life busting rocks."

"What's done is done, Leonardo. We can't undo it now. We got to work with what we got," said Lucero, trying to keep Rodríguez calm. "Look, I can make sure that the crate moves around the country and doesn't get delivered to Arica until we

---

[114] During the 1950s and 1960s, inflation averaged 31 percent per annum. See, for example, http://countrystudies.us/chile/58.htm

all can be there to pick it up. Eduardo and I can be in and out of town in a day, and you'll have your money, cold, hard cash, all in used United States currency.

"And besides, we've taken care of all the paperwork," Lucero continued in a soothing voice. "Everything was done according to Army regulations. We have the receipt from the appliance dealer, the receipt from the Dock Master that we'll give you, the other paperwork consigning the crate to the Fleet Warehouse in Talcahuano for shipment to Punta Arenas, and all. No one could ever suspect there's anything inside that crate except a new refrigerator built in the United States. And believe me, given what we found in those safe deposit boxes, no one's going to report a theft. The last thing they needs is the *Carabiñeros* to take an interest in their finances."

Rodríguez and Lucero continued to talk. Eventually, Rodríguez resigned himself to the situation.

"Well, I guess you're right. At this point, I don't have no choice."

Lucero restarted the engine. They pushed on, looking for seals that might have pulled themselves onto the ice.

Some twenty minutes later, Rodríguez again became agitated. Lucero cut the engine.

"Look, dammit, I'm the one that's taking all the risk here!" stammered Rodríguez. "If someone starts digging into that crate and finds the loot, it's my name that's on the manifest and shipping documents. And I'm not taking the fall for this by myself! You didn't give me a choice in the matter! I'm the one with the family who will have to sit on my share for a year while you two are off having a great time spending yours. I want $2 million in U.S. dollars, and some gold, too!"

Bellolio's face turned red. "You can't do that!" he shouted. Out of the corner of his eye, Lucero saw him reach for his switchblade. Their eyes locked. Lucero's stare convinced Bellolio to take his hand out of his pants pocket.

Lucero turned to Rodriquez and put his hands into the air, palms up. "All right, all right, what you say is true, Leonardo.

"Fair is fair. You and I go back a long ways, and we didn't give you a choice. You'll have your $2 million in U.S. currency and 300 gold U.S. $20 coins, too." He held up his left hand to silence Bellolio before the man could say anything.

"Let's go, Eduardo, we're running out of time. We have to bring back at least one seal or people are going to suspect that we was out here doing something more than hunting." He started the engine, using the lowest throttle setting to minimize the boat's wake.

The engine was operating at its quietest now, all the better for them to surprise seals that might be resting on icebergs in their path.

Slowly they made their way among the sea ice. The only sounds heard were the low, throaty sound of the engine's exhaust and ice scraping the bow and sides of the launch.

Turning to his right, Rodríguez spotted two forms, both long and gray, on an iceberg. He turned around and gestured wildly to Lucero and Bellolio with his arms to get their attention. Then, motioning with his head, he whispered loudly through cupped hands, "Over there! Over there! Weddell seals."[115]

The seals were lying on a flat, rectangular piece of ice about ten feet by fifteen feet in size. Rodríguez immediately signaled Lucero to kill the engine. As the launch slid silently past the

---

115 http://bloggingantarctica.blogspot.com/2006/12/seals.html

iceberg on which the seals lay, they awoke, and one slipped quietly into the water. As the other started to move toward the edge of the iceberg, Bellolio, ever impatient, picked up a rifle, turned quickly to his right, and without taking aim, shot it. Unfortunately, he only wounded the seal. As it lay writhing on the ice, blood spurting from a head wound, Rodríguez started swearing at Bellolio.

Turning to his right, Rodríguez spotted two forms, both long and gray, on an iceberg.[116]

"Just like you swabs! The only person safe when you have a rifle in your hands is the person you're shooting at! I guess the best way to put the thing out of its misery and, at the same time, attach a rope to him so we can tow him back to the base, is to get on the ice and put a knife through his heart."

Rodríguez motioned for Lucero to restart the engine and for Bellolio to take the boat back to the iceberg. Once it touched

116 Photo by author

the ice, Rodríguez jumped over the side with one end of a rope and knelt beside the seal. Unfortunately, what he did *not* see was Lucero throwing the coiled rope into the water while he motioned to Bellolio to back the boat away from the iceberg.

By the time Rodríguez had killed the seal and tied the rope around its neck, the launch was more than thirty feet from the iceberg and backing up at a good speed.

Rodríguez was stunned! “What are you doin’? Come back here. We need to drag this seal back to the base.”

“I’m sorry, Leonardo,” shouted Lucero, “but we can’t take any chances. I thought we could make this work, but you had to get greedy. I’m not sure that once we get everything back to your home in Arica, you will be able to keep your mouth shut long enough for us to get to Peru. So, we’re going to have to leave you here.”

Rodríguez jumped up and down on the ice and screamed. *“¡Bastardos! ¡Bastardos! ¡Ustedes se pudrirán en el infierno!”*[117]

Small ripples radiated from around the edges of the iceberg, rapidly carrying the sound of Rodríguez’s boots hitting the iceberg’s surface through the water toward the sensitive ears of any nearby orcas.[118]

Lucero was the first to spot them. A pod breached the surface 300 feet away to the port side of the launch.

He put his index finger into the air and made a circular motion with his hand, at the same time calling to Eduardo,

---

117 “Bastards! Bastards! You will rot in Hell!”

118 The speed of sound in seawater is approximately 1450 meters per second at 32 degrees Fahrenheit, which equates to 4756 feet per second (just under one mile per second). This is roughly four times the speed of sound in air.

"Turn the boat around . . . slowly. But get us away from here *now!*" Meanwhile, keeping the engine running at a low speed so as not to attract the orcas' attention, he used his compass to obtain a bearing on Base O'Higgins.

The pod continued moving toward the iceberg on which Rodriquez was standing. He saw them coming, and before he could steady himself, one of the killer whales put his head on the iceberg's edge, tipping it toward him and using his weight to break off a large piece.

Rodríguez dove for the surface of the ice and grabbed the seal, its body covered with blood, blood that now was oozing all over the ice and into the water. He took out his hunting knife and plunged it into the ice. This would give him more leverage in the event the orcas attempted to up-end the iceberg.

With the sun now shining brilliantly from above, the orca pod, looking up from below, interpreted the shadows they saw as coming from *two* seals lying on the ice.[119]

One by one the orcas placed their heads on the iceberg, attempting to use their weight to tip the 'seals' into the water. But by holding onto the dead seal, spreading his legs, and holding onto his knife, Rodríguez managed to maintain his position.

Two minutes passed.

Then, to his left, Rodríguez saw a wave coming toward the iceberg. This isolated 2-foot-high wave could only have been made by living creatures. He had heard stories about how killer

---

119 The orcas would not have smelled the seal's blood. Olfactory lobes of the brain and olfactory nerves are absent in all toothed whales, which indicates that they have no sense of smell at all. They rely fully on hearing and their eyesight to seek prey. http://www.scienceinformer.com/zoology/Killer-Whales.html

whales coordinate their actions to push a wall of water before them in an attempt to upset a small iceberg on which a seal or a penguin has taken refuge.[120] [121] *My God, the orcas are working together to create waves. They are trying to tip the iceberg so that I will be thrown into the water!* The wave passed under the iceberg, but it failed to dislodge either Rodríguez or the seal to which he now was desperately holding tight.

The sea became quiet. Rodríguez looked to his left, then to his right. *What the hell am I going to do?* He was panic-stricken. *"¡Lucero! ¡Hijo de puta! ¡Yo te mataré!"*[122]

For an instant he thought about how Lucero and Bellolio were going to explain his absence when they arrived at the base. *Maybe my commandante, working with the captain of the Lientur, will send a launch back and search for me, assuming they can determine where we are. How could they* not *search for me?*

Now, however, survival was *uppermost* in his mind.

What are *the orcas doing? Where are they?* His body was shaking uncontrollably, as much from fear as from the temperature of the ice and the water penetrating his heavy clothes.

He again looked left and right.

A minute passed.

Suddenly, out of the corner of his eye, he saw it . . . *a wall of water, a 15-ton, 4-foot-high wall of seawater!*

---

120 http://www.youtube.com/watch?v=oxDZW4k8tCY This disturbing footage shows a pod of orcas attempting to dislodge a seal from a small iceberg.

121 http://www.grupofalco.com.ar/pedefes/Visser%20et%20al%20 2008.%20Antarctic%20killer%20whales%20on%20ice%20-%20 Marine%20Mammals%20Science.pdf

122 "Lucero! You son of a prostitute! I will kill you!"

Rodríguez barely had time to comprehend what was happening when the wave hit, thrusting him and the dead seal into the air and down the backside of the ice into the water. Instantly he felt a sharp pain in his left chest, an excruciating pain that took his breath away. The numbing cold of the ice-laden water had stopped his heart. Before his hands could reach his chest, the jaws of a 6-ton killer whale clamped down on his waist. The orca's 3-inch-long teeth ripped through his clothes, the whale's jaws crushing his flesh and bones.

Shaking him violently, the killer dove instinctively for the depths with its prey, dragging Rodríguez's lifeless body down 200 feet to the bottom of the channel. Two other orcas took the seal, ripping it in half. Blood sprayed over the water and ice. The killing spree was over in less than ten seconds.

Except for seal blood on the ice and one of Rodríguez's gloves floating on the water, there were no signs of what had just happened. The orca pod disappeared into the ocean's depths. The only sounds were from sea water and small pieces of ice lapping against the side of the launch.

Lucero and Bellolio, hunched down in the launch, watched from a distance. They saw it all, every grizzly detail. Their faces were expressionless

"Well, I guess we were warned just in time," said Lucero. *"Quien es advertido en el tiempo es guardado."*[123] He took off his left glove, removed his parka hood, and combed his hair back with his fingers. Then he wiped his forehead with the back of his greasy parka sleeve. Putting his parka hood and glove back on, he took a deep breath, shrugged, and said matter of factly, "It simply wasn't going to work, was it?"

---

[123] "He who is warned in time is saved." Chilean proverb

"Now what do we do?" exclaimed Bellolio, throwing his hands into the air, always at a loss for answers.

"Well, we'll tell the story just as it happened. The enlisted men at the base already had one scare because of the orcas, so it wouldn't be a surprise to anyone that killer whales was still around. And after all, *Leonardo* was the one who suggested the hunt and who insisted on climbing out of the boat to finish off the seal.

"Yes, sir, Eduardo, we have to count ourselves lucky that the orcas, try as they might, were unable to tip us over after they finished off poor Leonardo. I tell you, we barely escaped with our lives. I think we both need to be checked out by bones[124] when we get back. My heart can't take much more of this!"

"Come on, Raul, this is serious! What are we gonna do about the refrigerator? If we don't do something, the Army will confiscate the crate and find the loot! And then, they will start working backwards, to the Port of Talcahuano!"

"Take it easy, Eduardo. The Army isn't going to do nothing. Do you think they are going to deprive his widow of the last gift her poor deceased husband, who died in the line of duty, I might add, bought for her?" asked Lucero rhetorically. "Never!"

"We'll just make some small changes to the storage and routing paperwork," he continued, "to delay the refrigerator's arrival in Arica until we can get there. I have a friend in Naval Supply who can take care of that. All we have to do is keep the damn thing moving around the country for a few weeks until you and me is sure of when we can arrive. Then, I'll have the crate delivered. We'll unpack it for poor Juanita—taking our property out first, of course—remove her old unit, move the

124 Navy slang for a doctor; sawbones

new refrigerator into her kitchen, and turn it on for the dear woman. It's the least we can do in honor of her late departed husband. After all, we went back a good number of years, you may recall."

Lucero was feeling smug. "We need to be in Arica anyway, to pay our respects to the widow Rodríguez. I'm sure that the Navy will give us leave at least for that, seeing as we was with the poor man when he met his Maker.

"Now, get us back to O'Higgins!" he commanded as he opened the engine's throttle and pointed toward the southeast. "I'm getting hungry."

X

Death Stalks The Expedition

With the *Piloto Pardo* and *Lientur* having left Base O'Higgins, the *Yelcho* at Arturo Prat in the South Shetlands, and a fourth ship, the *Lautaro* still in Punta Arenas, the only way for Grant and Ted to reach sites of geologic interest in the field was by using a small inflatable raft to move among the closer inshore islands.

Weather being as unpredictable as it was—a day could go from sunny to stormy in an hour—they could only get out into the field, on average, one of every three days. It was difficult paddling a raft to the various islands, not to mention fighting the fog, wind, waves, and ice. But they had no choice, and when conditions looked favorable, after alerting the base commandant and showing him on their maps where they would be working, they dragged their large yellow, inflatable raft to the dock and pushed off.

The islands comprised a broad range of rock types, ranging from basaltic to sedimentary. But what really excited Grant was the discovery of fossils on two islands close the base. The fossils were what he needed to determine the geologic age of the islands and to link their geology to the geology of another area he was studying in southern Chile. To him, these fossils were his Rosetta stone, the key to the success of his thesis.

The men logged, bagged, and tagged the rock samples and fossils, then, raced back to the base to get on the radio to the *Piloto Pardo*. The news that Grant had found the fossils for which he had been searching was welcome indeed, and Professor O'Mhaille was elated. All of his and Grant's work to date, including all their proposals to National Science Foundation and that federal organization's funding of Grant's research, had paid off, and the dividends were significant. Even David chimed in by radio from the *Yelcho*, offering his congratulations. It truly was a time for a celebration.

Amazing what you will do when you are bored, Ted thought, as he headed for the kitchen. The wind had been blowing at sixty miles per hour for two days, and other than venturing to his tent at night—if he even could define 'night', except by using his wristwatch—it was impossible to do anything outside. *Perhaps I can help the cook.* He went through the open door from the hallway leading to Sergeant Pedro Hidalgo's kitchen.

"Teodoro, did you come for more of my New Year cookies, amigo?" He knew Ted's sweet tooth well.

"No, I can't work today, so I thought I'd help you, if you want help."

"¡Por supuesto, amigo![125] Please, how would you like to bake a cake?"

Hidalgo handed Ted an apron, two boxes of slightly out-of-date Duncan Hines cake mix, a bowl, and place to work at his counter. *Just like home,* Ted thought. As a boy, he loved helping his mother in the kitchen, especially if he got to lick

125 "Of course, my friend!"

the mixing bowl when the last of the batter was poured into the cake tin.

"¿Hay algunos huevos de pollo?" asked Ted. "Any chicken eggs?"

Hidalgo laughed and waved Ted away, as if to say, *are you kidding? Here?*

So, without eggs, Ted baked what he thought were two pretty good examples of Duncan Hines chocolate cakes for the evening meal's dessert. But now, the thought of serving unadorned cakes bothered him.

"What about frosting, Hidalgo? Do you have any?"

Hidalgo pointed to the door at the back of the kitchen. "Try looking in the storage room. Perhaps there is something back there that you can use."

Ted pushed the door to the storeroom open and switched on the one naked 60-Watt lightbulb hanging from a cord stapled to the ceiling. In addition to several shelves containing foodstuffs, the room was filled with large wood crates, all consigned to what appeared to be the homes of Army personnel throughout Chile.

Ted had heard about the program in which civilian and military personnel who volunteer for duty in the Antarctic can purchase luxury foreign appliances without paying the exorbitant import taxes that otherwise would be levied on these goods by the Chilean government. The offer is extended on the condition that the appliances must accompany these personnel to Antarctica. Then, they are returned to Chile for delivery to their final destination when the Expedition ends and the personnel return home on leave. The incentive associated with this perk was sufficient to entice more than enough personnel from Chile's three military services to volunteer, year after year, for duty in the Antarctic. He recognized the names on the crates as those of the Army personnel assigned to Base O'Higgins.

One crate in particular caught his eye. It was in the back, tucked in a corner, not easily seen in the partial darkness of the storeroom. Before he even got to it, Ted saw that it was heavily reinforced with 1-inch plywood strips. Steel bands were wrapped around the crate at the top, middle, and bottom, firmly securing the four sides and ensuring that the container could weather even the worst physical abuse. Ted approached the crate and reached for it, as if by touching it he could get a sense of its contents. Then, he heard a voice behind him.

"What do you find so interesting about that crate, Señor Stone?"

Ted's heart stopped. He turned around slowly.

It was Javier, aka 'el Bigote',[126] the cook's helper. The thin mustache over his upper lip looked as if it had been applied using a black eyebrow pencil. Like many on the base, he made it his business to know everyone *else's* business.

"You startled me," said Ted, breathing a sigh of relief.

"Whatever is in that crate, señor, it must be made of pure gold . . . *oro puro*!" The Mustache patted the crate gently with his right hand. "Sergeant Major Salazar almost got a hernia moving this crate here from the dock. Thank God those two Navy non-coms helped us. Everybody is wondering what's in it.

126 Mustache

"Enlisted men will ship at least one large appliance down here if they can escape the taxes we have to pay on imported products! And the officers . . . *usted no tiene idea de las cosas que ellos envían acá.*[127] Still, I've never seen anything like this . . . so heavy!"

Ted shook his head side to side. "It's certainly a different way of doing business than I've ever heard of, Javier. I hope Rodríguez's wife will find some consolation when she finally receives this gift from her late husband. It really was tragic, what happened to him."

Thinking nothing more about the crate, Ted searched the cook's pantry for something that could be used to make frosting. And then it hit him: the National Science Foundation had provided a significant quantity of U.S. Army C-rations.[128] No matter that the food had been packed and sealed sometime in the 1950s *or earlier,* the food still was quite good, and on more than one occasion, Ted had opened a can of crackers and jam to enjoy a light afternoon snack in the field.

Braving the sixty mile per hour winds buffeting the base—*I must be nuts! The wind chill is at least -5 degrees Fahrenheit!*—Ted made a hurried trip to the Geophysical and Polar Research Center's crates stacked near their tent, dug through their rations, and found eight packets of what the U.S. Government termed 'soluble cocoa products'. Once back in the kitchen, he poured the contents into a large mixing bowl, added water, powered milk, a little vanilla, and *voilà, the perfect frosting!* Sergeant Hidalgo was amazed. Once the

---

127 " . . . you would not believe the things that they ship down here."

128 http://en.wikipedia.org/wiki/C-ration

frosting was spread on the cakes, he was even more impressed. But that was nothing compared to the accolades Ted received from the men, each of whom were given a small piece after the evening's meal. Now there were calls for Ted to assist Hidalgo with *all* desserts.

Ted laughed. *"¿Qué es lo que he hecho?"*[129] He knew that the cakes he had baked that afternoon would not be his last.

On the *Lientur,* Lucero received unsettling news.

"Eduardo," he whispered, when the two of them were alone at the stern, "meet me tonight at 6 bells[130] on the port side of the storage compartment forward of the engine room. We need to talk. *¡Tenemos un problema!*" [131]

When everyone had settled down for the night, the two men met below deck, concealed by boxes and crates strapped to tie points on the hull, deck, and overhead.

Lucero looked around to make sure no one was in the compartment. Then he whispered, "I received a 'condolence' message from Gabriel Osorio—*Chief Warrant Officer Osorio*—this afternoon. You remember me talking about him. We was on that rescue effort with the Norwegian relief ship *MS Tottan* that evacuated personnel from several sites occupied by French Antarctic researchers back in 1952.[132] [133] [134] We both

---

129 "What have I done?"

130 11:00 PM

131 "We have a problem!"

132 Includes trip to Kerguelen Island, 9 February 1952-19 March 1952, relief Expedition. See http://www.austehc.unimelb.edu.au/guides/lawp/LAWP002.htm (Antarctica (Heard and Macquarie Islands) 1952)

133 http://www.aad.gov.au/default.asp?casid=27177

134 http://www.south-pole.com/aspp109.htm

was assigned to the *Lautaro* back then. It was Hell! We lost two overboard in that storm off Kerguelen Island . . . never even had a chance to look for 'em, not that it would have done any good. They probably was drowned within seconds of hitting the water. Terrible thing it was.

"Well, seeing as how he's now in Navy Records and all, he kinda watches out for me, and I do him a favor now and then, if you know what I mean. Well, a few days ago, he sends me this radiogram telling me how fortunate it was that I didn't suffer the same fate as that poor unfortunate friend of mine, Rodríguez. The tragedy is all the talk in Santiago. Well, then he says that there's been a lot of interest shown in Rodríguez as well as in you and me by someone in Internal Affairs, so maybe someone was fixing to give us medals or something.

"So, I send him a radiogram, casual like, and I say, 'That's very interesting, Gabe. Can you find out who has been looking into our records. Maybe we can help them if they need some information,' I tell him. I have to be careful so Sparks[135] don't suspect nothing."

"What do you think is going on?" asked Bellolio.

"Well, Gabe comes back today and says that he was having drinks with another chief warrant officer, one who works in Internal Affairs. They was at that bar down near Navy Headquarters—you know the one—last night after work. They are old shipmates going back many years and watch each other's backs closely. The guy in Internal Affairs was the one who helped Gabe and me cover our tracks years ago when Internal Affairs was closing in on us after we took those supplies from

[135] The ship's radio operator

the Fleet Warehouses in Punta Arenas and Valparaiso, and shipped them to Santiago via various routes.

"Anyway, based on what Gabe asked him a day earlier, this friend tells him that those inquiries about Rodríguez, you, and me actually started coming in several months ago from someone on the *Pardo*.

"And then this guy, the one Gabe is talking to, says, 'But not long ago, the inquiries started coming from the *Lientur*.' He's telling me all this, nice and casual like, saying things like '*maybe you want to find the person on the* Lientur *who is looking at your records and see if you can help him.*'"

"So, what does that *mean?*" whispered Bellolio, throwing his arms into the air.

Lucero looked like he wanted to grab Bellolio by his head and shake him until his teeth fell out. "Oh, for *God's* sake, Eduardo, do I have to spell every damn thing out for you? It means that someone on this ship has picked up our trail. Someone has tied us to Rodríguez and probably to the stolen merchandise."

Bellolio reached for his knife. "Tell me who it is! *¡Yo lo mataré!*"[136]

"Don't be a fool, Eduardo! There is plenty of time to deal with this. My guess is, if the inquiries came first from the *Pardo* and now they're coming from here, there is only one person who could be behind an investigation—Commander Barbudo."

"Okay, okay . . . then, what *are* we going to do?"

"Now? Nothing. If Barbudo had anything, we'd already be in the brig. But sooner or later, he's gonna figure things out. So, at some point, you or I will have to make sure that the commander

---

[136] "I will kill him!"

has a little, ah, shall we say, *accidente*, which, unfortunately, will be fatal. We just have to find the right time and place to make it happen.

"My guess is, with you or me being out in the launches with the *gringo*[137] scientists, sooner or later the commander will join a shore party, just to relieve the boredom from being on the *Lientur*. That's when we'll strike. Whatever we do, we have to make sure they will never find his body."

"Ted, throw me the rock pick,[138] would you?"

Grant had just stepped out of their inflatable raft onto a small island located some 100 feet off the Continental Glacier. He climbed quickly up the ice-free surface as a broad ocean swell washed over the area where he had been standing. Ted was attempting to hold the raft in position just off the island, and at the same time, find the pick, which Grant had left in one of the backpacks aboard the raft. Because of bad weather, this was the first time in three days that they had even been able to get into the field. Both the *Yelcho* and *Lientur* were committed elsewhere in the area of operations, so there was nothing they could do but explore the islands close to the base. They were anxious to have something to show for the day's effort.

A large swell moved the raft away from the island, and as Ted attempted to toss the pick underhand to Grant, a gentle wave tipped the boat slightly, causing him to undershoot the target. The pick hit the island and bounced into the ocean.

"Dammit!" Ted yelled. "You'd think by now I could at least toss a pick to you!"

---

137 Denotes a foreigner, or in this case, American scientists

138 http://en.wikipedia.org/wiki/Geologist's_hammer

They did not have a second pick of that type with them, and it would take quite a while to row back to the base for another.

"Do you think you can 'fish' for it the water? Is there a nylon cord in the raft?" yelled Grant.

"Well, there may be, but getting it looped around the pick is not going to be easy in this surf. There's only one way to get it back," yelled Ted. "I'm going to reach down and grab it!"

"Are you out of your mind?" yelled Grant. "That's too big a risk. You know what can happen to your body in this climate, especially if it's exposed to the elements!"

"Do you have a better idea? Look, the air temperature is in the mid-40s, the sun is out. I can reach down and grab it between swells, and we'll be back at work in ten minutes. From what I can see, it appears to be about three feet below the surface, perhaps a little less. The water's nice and clear, though a wee bit cold, I'm sure! [139]

"Watch this!" said Ted as he started to unsnap his parka.

"Right, watch this. The two most dangerous words in the English language," said Grant. "You're kidding, aren't you?

"That water is below freezing. Just dunking your head and upper body in it for even a few seconds could shock your system and disrupt your heart's rhythm. Then what? The last thing we need on this Expedition is another death! I don't want to take you home in a wooden box!"

---

[139] Antarctic sea water varies between about 35 degrees F (2 degrees C) and 28 degrees F (-2 degrees C, the approximate freezing point of sea water) over the course of a year. See, for example: http://www.coolantarctica.com/Antarctica%20fact%20file/antarctica%20environment/weather.htm

"Listen, every New Year's Day, members of the Milwaukee Polar Bear Club take a dip in Lake Michigan at Bradford Beach![140] They haven't lost anybody yet to the cold water, so I figure the odds are in my favor! We Milwaukeeans are a hardy lot!"

Before Grant could say another word, Ted stripped off his parka, insulated vest, heavy woolen shirt, and insulated undershirt. He brought the raft to the edge of the island. Wiping some seawater on his hair, face, and chest, he waited until the next swell passed. Then, holding tight to a rope tie on the top of the raft with his right hand, he took a deep breath, ducked his upper body under the water, and grabbed the pick on the first try.

He surfaced triumphantly, holding the pick high above his head.

"Whoa! It's cold!" he yelled, spitting seawater. He was breathing fast and hard, but other than that, was no worse for wear.

"That was crazy, Ted!" Nevertheless, Grant was elated that Ted had retrieved the pick. Without it, there would have been no way for them to obtain rock and fossil samples from the island that day.

Ted put the pick on the bottom of the raft, used his shirt to dry himself, then put on his insulated underwear, insulated vest, and parka. The woolen shirt, which he had wrung out, would have to dry in the sun before he could wear it, but with the sun rising and the wind calm, he did not need it.

"Do you want to try throwing it to me again?" asked Grant, grinning.

---

140 http://www.jsonline.com/news/milwaukee/36906624.html

"Not on your life!" He rowed the raft closer to the island. "This time, you'll have to come down here and get it!"

"You do know that we can't keep working this way," said Grant as he gingerly inched toward the edge of the island, toward where Ted was rowing their raft. "We've already gone far beyond any reasonable distance from the base to get the samples we need. If anything had happened, your little episode in the water notwithstanding, there would have been no way for anyone to have helped us . . . if they even knew exactly where to look!

"If I can't convince the Navy to provide support for at least a week, I will never be able to gather the rock and fossil samples I need to complete my thesis. I'll talk with the base commander when we return to O'Higgins and see if he can intercede on my behalf."

"Ted, wake up!"

It was Grant. The time was 4:10 AM; the day, January 21st. Grant already was dressed and had just eaten an early morning breakfast at the base. Ted never heard him leave.

He crawled back into the tent. "The *Yelcho* came up from Base GGV last night!" he exclaimed excitedly. "The ship has been maneuvering in the channel offshore for the last six hours because of the ice."

The fact was, even if they could have anchored—and given the smooth ocean floor in front of the base, that would have been impossible—the presence of icebergs required that the ship's crew constantly alter the *Yelcho's* position to avoid a collision that might damage its hull.

The presence of icebergs required that the ship's crew constantly alter the *Yelcho's* position to avoid a collision that might damage its hull.[141]

For more than two weeks Grant had practically begged on bended knee for the flotilla to send a ship to O'Higgins to support his research. Without access to a motorized launch, his and Ted's excursions to the offshore islands and down the coast of the North Antarctic Peninsula were limited to less than a quarter of a mile, if that, because of the vagaries of the weather, the rough seas, and ice. If Grant had any hope at all of reaching the outer islands or rock outcrops on the Continental Glacier farther south on the Peninsula, their *only* possible source of transportation would be one of the Expedition's ships.

According to the *Yelcho's* captain, he could provide Grant with support for four days, and he suggested that they begin as soon as possible. The weather was excellent, with clear skies

141 Photo by BigStockPhoto

and no wind. The sea was quiet, and though packed with ice, he did not foresee a problem in moving about the area.

Grant, who already had most of the equipment and supplies packed, suggested a field trip to one of the islands in a large group located about three miles to the northeast of the base.[142] The captain agreed, and with the help of two Navy enlisted men, Grant and Ted soon loaded everything they needed into a motorized launch for the short trip to the *Yelcho*.

Among the equipment Ted carried with him in a canvas bag was a small, War-surplus[143] high-frequency radio transceiver. It was tuned to the agreed-upon call frequency in one of the maritime radio bands. Before leaving, Grant and Ted had agreed to check in with the *Yelcho's* radio operator every four hours once they were on the island. The antenna was a simple insulated wire some sixty feet in length that Ted could let out onto the snow, and the transmitter, which ran no more than two Watts input, was expected to load easily at a frequency of 6300 kHz.

It was a short voyage from Base O'Higgins to the island group to the northeast, and within thirty minutes of arriving, Navy enlisted men had a motorized launch in the water, already loaded with Grant and Ted's equipment and supplies. The launch, with a crew of four, including the helmsman and the motorman, as well as Grant and Ted aboard, reached a small pebble beach in five minutes, and once beached, was unloaded

---

142 The National Science Foundation later would name these islands the Wisconsin Islands. They are located at 63°17'S, 57°51'W. The group comprises a dozen or more small rocky islands that lie 1 mile NE of Largo Island in the NE part of the Duroch Islands. They are named after the University of Wisconsin-Madison.

143 World War II

quickly. The launch then returned to the *Yelcho*, which returned to the waters off Base O'Higgins, there to wait in the event Grant and Ted needed assistance.

The area above the beach still was covered by two feet of snow, so the two men immediately set about erecting their two-man tent there. Once their sleeping bags had been unrolled and the radio positioned, with its antenna extended out of the tent's flap-covered opening and across the snow, they set out to explore the island. To their north, at a distance of 300 feet, was a large Gentoo penguin rookery, but the opportunity for taking pictures would have to wait. For now, gathering rock and fossil samples was uppermost in the men's minds.

They had been working three hours when they both noticed that the wind was picking up.

"Looks like clouds are moving into the area," said Grant, looking up. "Perhaps we have a storm moving up from the south, up the Bransfield Strait. Maybe we should start heading back to the tent now, just in case. I wouldn't want to get caught out here in the open if the weather changes all of a sudden."

Ted agreed. "The way the weather changes down here, you never know what's going to happen from one minute to the next. Besides, we have to meet a radio schedule in less than an hour, so it's probably best to go now and finish the paperwork for these samples in the tent. If we do have a storm, we'll be safe and out of the weather."

Before the men could reach their tent, the sky turned jet black, and the wind, which minutes earlier had been calm, jumped to more than forty miles per hour, driving the snow before it horizontally. They dove into the tent, shutting the flaps just as the wind increased even more, with gusts reaching sixty miles per hour.[144]

A call on the radio brought responses both from the base as well as the *Yelcho.*

The men let the two radio operators know that they were okay.

"Unfortunately," said the *Yelcho's* operator, "the barometer has fallen steeply. We are registering barometric pressures around 980 millibars now.[145] This will be a severe storm."

The *Yelcho's* operator went on to say that, while they did not know how long the storm would last, there was no way, under the circumstances, that they could come back now to take them off the island. They would have to spend the night there, and the *Yelcho* would return in the morning, if the storm had abated, to take them back to Base O'Higgins.

Ted told the operator they understood the situation and would meet the next schedule, as they had agreed. Sleeping through the schedule was not a concern; the howling wind and sound of snow and sleet hitting the tent kept them awake all night.

By the next morning, a foot of new snow had fallen. When Grant and Ted finally cleared the entrance to their tent and were able to crawl out, the sky was bright blue, the sun was out, and a light breeze was blowing in from the ocean.

"Well," joked Grant, "that's quite a change from yesterday!"

Ted radioed the *Yelcho.* The operator indicated the combination of high winds, low visibility, and icebergs in the

---

144 Winds gusts to 80 miles per hour were reported at Base O'Higgins.

145 At sea level, standard air pressure is 1013.25 millibars.

channel near Base O'Higgins forced them to take the ship far out to sea to avoid collisions that could have damaged her hull. The captain estimated it would take at least six hours for the ship to return and pick them up.

Grant and Ted proposed waiting five hours, checking the *Yelcho's* progress at that time, and if everything was going according to plan, breaking down the tent and preparing to be picked up. The ship's operator said the captain agreed with that plan.

Five hours passed. The *Yelcho* now was within 45 minutes of the base, and the signal from the ship was strong. She was making good time. The radio operator cautioned, however, that, based on radio reports from Greenwich Island, another storm was moving toward O'Higgins, and that Grant and Ted should be prepared to leave the island as soon as the ship arrived.

The two men immediately set about rolling up their sleeping bags, breaking down and packing the tent, and packing everything, including the samples they collected, in the canvas bags they brought with them.

In less than an hour from the time of their last radio contact, the *Yelcho* appeared offshore. Unfortunately, the wind had picked up again, the sky had darkened, and the surf presented a challenge to the crew that was bringing a launch to the beach. The helmsman did an excellent job of beaching the launch, and while the motorman and another sailor held tight to lines that kept the craft onshore, Grant, Ted, and another sailor moved all of the canvas bags into the launch as quickly as possible. Unfortunately, one bag, which contained the radio transceiver, slipped into the water, and both the radio and the rock samples were completely soaked.

"I'm not worried about the samples," yelled Grant, "but what are we going to do about the radio? Without that, we could be in real trouble the next time we're in the field."

"I'll have to work on that when we get to the base," shouted Ted, his voice barely rising above the wind, which by now had climbed above thirty miles per hour. "If we don't get the salt water flushed out of it and get it cleaned up, we'll never be able to use it again!"

By the time they got the launch back to the *Yelcho,* the wind exceeded forty miles per hour, the sky again was black, and the barometer was falling. Grant and Ted climbed a rope ladder to reach the deck while the ship's crew brought their equipment to the deck. Once the launch and its crew had been retrieved, the ship began turning around.

"I don't think we're heading for Base O'Higgins," said Ted to Grant.

Ted looked over the port railing. "We're heading out to sea!"

The men headed into the *Yelcho's* cabin and walked toward the bridge, where they met Capitán Julio Pérez. *"Lo siento caballeros, pero nos estamos dirigiendo a la Base Prat. Nosotros no podemos quedarnos aquí."*[146]

"Unbelievable," said Grant. "This is my second year working in this area, and I never have seen a storm blow up so quickly!"

With no place to anchor and the icebergs posing a significant threat to the ship, there was no option but to run for shelter at Base Prat in the Shetland Islands. As the ship

[146] "I am sorry, gentlemen, but we are headed to Base Prat. We can not stay here."

moved west, the seas got steadily worse. By 6:00 PM, the waves exceeded twenty-five feet in height, with an occasional rogue wave reaching thirty-five feet. Grant and Ted were assigned bunks just behind the bridge. Grant immediately strapped himself in, using one of his wading boots as a convenient place to deposit the contents of his stomach when his seasickness got the better of him. There was no way that he could make it to the ship's railing, much less stand.

Except for the helmsman, strapped into the chair positioned behind the ship's wheel, everyone stayed in their bunks. Anything not securely fastened to the wall or a table was thrown into the air, and the decks were littered with books, pieces of a typewriter that had been thrown into a bulkhead when a rogue wave slammed into the ship, shards of porcelain, and other objects.

With great difficulty, Ted clawed his way through the passageway to the bridge. Holding on to the helmsman's chair with both hands, he watched as the ship tilted up at a thirty degree angle, paused for a moment, then, crashed down with a thunderous clap, only to plow through the next wave, which completely washed over the entire bow of the ship. At times, the sea water and spray washing against the bridge's windows was so thick that it was impossible to see the bow.

The ship rolled incessantly from port to starboard and back again, to angles that at times seemed as high as 45 degrees.

"¿Señor, cuál es el ángulo donde el barco ya no va a poder estabilizarse?"[147] asked Ted, with some trepidation in his voice.

---

147 "Señor, at what angle will the ship fail to recover?"

The seaman laughed. *"Aún tenemos manera de estabilizarnos, mi amigo. El punto sin retorno es sesenta y tres grados."*[148]

Somehow, Ted was not reassured. He returned to his bunk, clung to a chain on the wall to keep from being thrown on the deck, and waited. He needed to go to the head around midnight, but could not even stand, so violent was the motion of the ship.

Finally, when he no longer could wait, he carefully made his way down the stairs to the lower deck and into the bow of the ship, where he found two toilets fastened to a bulkhead. Next to each were two stainless steel bars that extended up from the deck to the overhead. *Wow, standing here is like trying to relieve yourself from the back of a bucking bronco!* What choice did he have? He held on to one of the bars for dear life.

Ted finally made it back to his bunk, where he spent the rest of the night. By the next morning, they were safely in the harbor at Base Prat. The 'night of hell' had passed, the sky had cleared, and the ship was safe.

After breakfast, Ted took a launch from the *Yelcho* to the base, and together with the ship's radio operator, Leading Rate Roberto Vicuña, approached the base's communications officer about using his facility to repair the University's radio transceiver that had fallen into the ocean.[149]

---

[148] "We have a way to go yet, my friend. The point of no return is sixty-three degrees."

[149] Salt water residue would ruin the radio because of its corrosive and conductive nature.

The communications officer, Navy Lieutenant Alonso Benítez, was happy to make his facility available and offered *his* assistance as well. Benítez was a graduate of multiple technical radio courses at both U.S. *and* Chilean Navy communications schools. He had more than seven years of experience with all types of high-frequency radio communications equipment, including the type Ted was using, and was *exactly* the person needed to help restore the University's radio.

Working together, the three men began by taking the radio out of its canvas bag, removing the chassis from its cabinet, and disconnecting the two batteries, which they discarded. They removed the tubes, washed them in a mild, warm soapy solution, rinsed them in distilled water, and dried them on a clean towel. Using warm, distilled water and a stiff bristle brush, they completely cleaned the chassis, making sure that every possible place where saltwater could have penetrated was thoroughly drenched.

When they were finished, Benítez took the transceiver to the kitchen, where he "baked" it in an oven at 100 degrees for one hour. With the unit dry, the entire chassis, top and bottom, was sprayed with a non-lubricating contact cleaner to drive any residual salt and other contaminants from the equipment. A good blast with compressed air removed any remaining residue that somehow might have escaped the cleansing process to this point.

Finally, after Ted sprayed all switch contacts, tube sockets, and tube pins with a lubricating contact cleaner, the men reassembled the radio.

Fortunately, the base had a set of spare batteries, and once they were installed, the transceiver immediately came to life.

"Let's let the radio idle for four hours," said Benítez, "just to make certain that our efforts have been successful."

The equipment passed with flying colors!

The only remaining step now was to place the radio back in its canvas bag, which also had been washed in a mild soapy solution, rinsed, and dried.

Throwing the radio over his back, Ted and the *Yelcho's* radio operator bid farewell to the lieutenant, thanking him profusely for his help, and left. They were fortunate to reach the beach just as a launch was about to leave the island.

Because of a major storm, the *Yelcho* was unable to return to Base O'Higgins until January 29th. By then, the seas were calm, there was little wind, and the sky overhead was cloudless. Other than the usual icebergs and other floating ice, there were no impediments in her path, and the ship arrived in the waters off the base. The captain said that he had orders to turn south that evening and set course for Base GGV, where one of the Chilean scientists had requested assistance. But in the meantime, he would direct his men to provide support to Grant and Ted for the purpose of making one trip to a nearby island, Isle Kopaitic, which they had yet to explore.

With a motor launch in the water, the captain gave instructions to the helmsman that he first was to take Grant and Ted to the dock so they could drop off the samples they were carrying, as well as any other equipment they did not need, including the refurbished radio, and pick up new sample bags and other equipment. While at the dock, First Sergeant Quesada, whose responsibility it was to feed the dogs, asked the motorman if he and an enlisted man could accompany them to the island. "The base is running low on seal meat for the dogs. We are getting desperate. I am hoping that we can shoot at least one seal while the scientists are collecting rock samples. We can tow the seal back to the base behind the motor launch."

The motorman radioed the ship for permission, and a few minutes later, the ship's radio operator called back, stating that the captain agreed to the plan.

The launch set out for Isle Kopaitic, the largest of a number of islands in the group northwest of the base. The island proved rich in rock varieties, and Grant found examples of two more fossil species similar to species he had found in South America, something that left him speechless.

Meanwhile, Sergeant Quesada and the enlisted man accompanying him came across a large elephant seal on a small piece of ice 300 feet down the beach from where the launch had been brought in. He shot the seal through the head, killing it instantly. The enlisted man tied a long nylon cord around the seal's head, and they waited for the launch.

Once everyone was back in the boat, the launch moved down the beach to pick up the seal. The sergeant and the enlisted man pulled the seal into the water and tied the line to one of the cleats at the rear of the launch. The helmsman then set course southeast, toward the base, the dead seal trailing behind.

They had gone about a mile when, without warning, a large orca more than ten feet long rose out of the water, and in one pass, took the entire seal, snapping the nylon cord in the process. So great was the orca's weight, and so strong its bite, that the mere act of taking the seal caused the boat to stop dead in the water for a split second.

The crew and passengers were stunned. When the motorman recovered his composure, he pushed the throttle to the limit.

"¡No me importa si los malditos perros se muren de hambre, yo nunca iré a cazar focas otra vez!" cried Sergeant Quesada, his whole body shaking from the ordeal.[150] "And I will *never* set foot on anything smaller than the *Lientur*, either!" shouted the sergeant, shaking his fist in the air.

There simply is no way for Man to overcome Nature, Ted reflected. *We may think that we are prepared for the worst, that we can anticipate the challenges we will face; make plans to mitigate the risks; take precautions; sail in vessels built for these waters; bring with us the clothes and tools we need to accomplish our work; avoid endeavors that put men and their ships in harm's way.*

And then, the unexpected happens! She's always out there, waiting. Nature, *in all Her many* unpredictable, deceitful *Earthly manifestations: winds that can top eighty miles per hour . . . some that roar, driving rain, sleet, and snow horizontally, blotting out the hand in front of your face . . . others that shriek, driving waves to heights of fifty feet and more, swallowing bows of ships, if not entire ships, as they plunge from crest to trough.*

What are we to make of Her alien domain: the Frozen Continent at the Bottom of the World with its mantle, Ice? Enveloping, looming over, and dominating the landscape . . .

---

150 "I don't care if the damn dogs starve to death, I will never go seal hunting again!"

melting, cracking, separating, inching inexorably toward the sea, calving in thunderous convulsions that send thousands of tons of ice and snow pouring down from great heights, creating walls of water and ice that threaten, attack, and overwhelm anything in their paths.

And then there are Her intelligent, silent killers of the deep that can rise up and take man and mammal alike without warning, only to disappear just as quickly, ready to strike again another day.

Scott was right; "Great God! This is an awful place!" [151]

At 2:00 AM, February 6th, the 'day' dawned bright and sunny. Ted could not sleep. He took off his eye shade, carefully got out of his sleeping bag, put on his clothes, grabbed his boots, and quietly stole out of the tent so as not to awake Grant. The dogs were quiet, and it appeared everyone was asleep on the base. The only sound heard was a lone skua on its way to a nearby penguin rookery in search of prey.

While pulling on his boots, Ted looked up toward the mountain that jutted out of the Continental Glacier to the southeast of the base. To his utter amazement, he saw two sleddog teams working their way down the glacier toward O'Higgins. *This is interesting,* he thought; *we've yet to have visitors, but even so, I would have expected any we* did *to arrive by sea.*

He ran to the base kitchen, grabbed a couple of biscuits to nibble on while he hiked up the glacier, and ran out the

151 Captain Robert F. Scott, British Royal Navy Officer and Explorer, upon reaching the South Pole in 1912

door and down the hill to a point near the dock. Crossing over the rocks that linked the small peninsula on which the base was located to the North Antarctica Peninsula, he carefully climbed over the ice to the top of the glacier. Once there, he started walking toward the teams, which by now were making considerable progress in their run down the mountain toward him.

Within twenty minutes they met. The dogteam drivers shouted "Down!" and the dogs immediately sat on the snow-covered glacier. Ted introduced himself, as did the four men. They were British Antarctic Survey scientists attached to the British Base D at Hope Bay,[152] which was located at the very tip of the North Antarctic Peninsula. *Well, it's comforting to speak English again,* thought Ted, even though his Spanish was getting better by the day.

Mike Dawson, the driver of the lead dog team, shed his thick gloves. Taking out a pack of *Sobranie Black Russians*, he offered everyone a cigarette. Ted declined, with thanks. The others declined as well, saying they had to feed and water the dogs, a task to which they immediately turned.

Dawson pulled off his hood, revealing a full head of bright red hair with a bushy beard and mustache of the same color. In his early thirties, he stood six feet tall with rugged features weathered by the Antarctic winds. His skin, once fair, had been burned bright red by the sun despite the generous covering of suntan lotion on his face and the protective cover over his nose. The highly silvered Polaroid sun glasses protecting his

---

152 http://www.antarctica.ac.uk/about_bas/our_history/stations_and_refuges/hope_bay.php The base, British Base D, was abandoned in February, 1964.

eyes made him a creature from outer space. Everything he wore was absolutely required for his survival. Like Ted, he was dressed in a gray parka, heavy pants, and work boots. Several layers of insulated clothing padded his lean body, giving him the flexibility to shed garments as the sun rose, taking the temperature with it.

Dawson flipped a cigarette out of the pack, snapped off the gold foil filter, and tapped the other end on the back of his left hand, packing the tobacco tight. Putting the packed end between his lips, he flicked his Ronson lighter once, cupped his hands, and lit the cigarette. *What a ritual!* Ted observed.

Drawing on the cigarette, Dawson took a deep breath and exhaled. Ted had given up smoking two months before the trip to Antarctica, but still, to him, nothing smelled as tempting as the odor of cigarette smoke in the crisp Antarctic air.

"Well," Dawson remarked, now in a pensive mood, "it's good to rest for a few minutes!" He picked a speck of tobacco off his tongue. "This is my sixth year on the ice, and it doesn't get any easier! We're on an 800-mile trek from Hope Bay down the Peninsula to measure ice thickness, elevations, annual snow accumulations, and other ice features. We knew our traverse would swing us near Base O'Higgins, but didn't plan to stop because of our tight schedule. What are you up to?"

Ted regaled him and the others with what had been happening to them since they departed from Punta Arenas, how the weather had pretty much put Grant's and his scientific endeavors behind schedule. "The tragic death of

First Sergeant Rodríguez didn't help, either. Now, no one from the base will take us out to the islands. We'll have to wait for the Chilean Navy if we're going to get the assistance we need."

"We heard about that accident," said Mike, drawing on his cigarette. "Bad luck, that. I've seen orcas force seals from the ice on several occasions. I've seen leopard seals[153] do it, too. It's not a pretty sight. Just a word to the wise, mate. Don't *ever* step out onto a piece of floating ice. If an orca doesn't get you, there's always the possibility that a leopard seal will, especially if you're close to a penguin colony!"

The five men rambled on about their lives and work in the Antarctic, their challenges and their triumphs, their difficulties and their successes. All agreed that the exhilaration that came from testing their mettle against Nature was what drove them day after day to meet and overcome the hardships they faced.

Several minutes had passed when Dawson happened to glance to his left, over the Bransfield Strait. The clouds, thickening and purplish-black, were ominous. "I think we need to move on, Ted," he said, a worried look crossing his face. "A storm is approaching." The wind rose rapidly, blowing smoke from the Black Russian straight back behind him. "This is a surprise," he said. "The last weather report I received from Base B on Deception three hours ago called only for a slight increase in the winds on the Peninsula today.

---

153 Leopard seals' main source of food is penguins and they can often be seen cruising in the vicinity of Adélie, Chinstrap, and Gentoo colonies. Their only known natural predator is the Killer Whale. See http://www.antarcticconnection.com/antarctic/wildlife/seals/leopard.shtml

You can't trust a damn thing down here from one minute to the next!"

Dawson immediately dropped the cigarette butt, pushed it into the ice with the toe of his boot, and hurriedly pulled his parka hood around his head. They said their goodbyes as the dogteam drivers shouted "Up!" to the dogs.

At the last minute, Ted shouted, "Wait, I have a question. One quick question!"

The drivers commanded their dogs to sit and turned to Ted, quizzical looks on their faces.

"I couldn't help noticing that your dogs are perfectly behaved . . . no fights, no baiting, no snarling . . . just two well-trained teams with each animal pulling his weight. Every time we try to harness the dogs at O'Higgins, we spend most of our time separating them. It's just a nightmare getting them to pull a sled, much less harnessing a full team. What's the key to *your* success?"

"Well, besides the expert, personalized training we provide to our dogs," said Dawson, an assertion that made everyone laugh, "all of the dogs on each of our teams are related to one another. They are fathers, mothers, brothers, or sisters. The younger ones started pulling small sleds at four months, and each was harnessed next to an older dog to teach the younger one teamwork. You can see the results!

"The Chileans use dogs of several different sizes and breeds, some they probably grabbed off the streets of Santiago. No wonder the dogs fight each other. You're lucky they aren't missing parts of their ears before you can separate them! Frankly, I wouldn't waste a pound of meat on the whole lot!"

Ted shook his head from side to side. "Unfortunately, one man at O'Higgins already has lost his life hunting seals for the meat needed to feed those mongrels."

Dawson shook his head as well. And then, the two dogsled drivers shouted "Up," the dogs leapt to their feet, and with shouts of "Hike," the two teams charged up the western flank of the mountain toward the site of their next encampment.

From afar, Ted admired the perfect timing of the powerful teams, the sled runners gliding efficiently across the snow, the scene itself a portrait of Antarctic *survival.* Dawson turned and waved a powerful gloved hand in farewell.

Dawson turned and waved a powerful gloved hand in farewell.[154]

Grant and Ted continued to explore the islands close to Base O'Higgins while they awaited the arrival of a ship that could extend their 'reach' to the outer islands or to the south,

[154] Photo by author

along the Antarctic Peninsula. Their spirits were buoyed by the successes achieved, despite their inability to get into the field as often as planned. Grant had mapped large portions of their work area, and the variety of rocks collected as well as the fossils uncovered would provide the samples needed to write a defensible doctoral thesis in Cretaceous sedimentation.

Meanwhile, David was achieving similar successes in the collection of the rock samples he needed for his doctoral work as well as the work he was doing to help Ted establish a new gravity network in the Chilean Antarctic. It was shaping up to be a banner austral summer in the Antarctic for the University of Wisconsin contingent! *Finally, things are starting to go our way,* Ted thought.

He thought, too, about everything that had happened since they arrived . . . how Rodríguez, a man he only met once, had suffered a horrible death almost immediately after their arrival at O'Higgins . . . how the captains of the *Piloto Pardo* and the *Lientur* both put launches into the water and searched the area where Lucero and Bellolio said that they had been hunting seals, only to find nothing . . . how they expected to find nothing . . . how they had to make the effort, according to Captain Muñoz of the *Lientur* . . . and how Captain Muñoz took the Army chaplain from O'Higgins to the site where Rodríguez was thought to have died so that the chaplain could offer a prayer for the dead.

And what about the constant array of problems they faced that were related to the weather, problems that severely limited Grant's and his research activities in the field? *Maybe things are looking up. If only we could get a little more support from the Chilean Navy, we could finish the field work on a high note!*

Without a Chilean naval vessel, it had been impossible for Grant and Ted to explore beyond the few islands close to Base O'Higgins, ground that they had been over many times. The additional days lost because of weather also reduced the opportunities available to explore areas that Grant thought would prove rich in rocks and fossils—areas that could provide missing pieces to a geologic jigsaw puzzle that was rapidly coming together for him in the form of his dissertation.

Grant's prayers for support were answered on February 10th when, late in the day, the *Lientur* appeared in the waters off the base, bringing with it needed supplies and mail. Captain Muñoz paid his respects to the base commandant, then greeted Grant and Ted.

"Now that we are nearing the end of the Expedition, my friends," said the captain, "the Comodoro has ordered me to provide whatever support you may need in the field. When you have finished your work, I am then to bring you to the South Shetland Islands in preparation for the final voyage home."

Grant wasted no time in providing the captain with a plan. "Captain Muñoz, first, Ted and I want to thank you for your support. Without you and your crew, I'm not sure that it would be possible for us to complete our work this year."

"It is our pleasure, Señor Morris. How can we be of service?"

"Here is a map showing the areas where we want to perform work south of Base O'Higgins, along the North Antarctic Peninsula. As you see, I have identified several points at which I would prefer to land on the way to Base GGV.

"Here," said Grant, pointing to a beach several miles south of the base, "is one place that I would like to go inland several thousand feet on the Continental Glacier. I need to explore an outcrop discovered two years ago by the British Antarctic Survey."

"Let me review this plan with my executive officer. I will give you my answer in the morning. In the meantime, I suggest that you and Señor Stone prepare to be at sea with me for the next ten days . . . perhaps longer, if the weather does not cooperate."

That night, Ted dozed off, hoping that finally, their luck had changed for the good. Suddenly, he had a strange sense of foreboding . . . nothing specific, really, just an uncomfortable feeling in the pit of his stomach that something was about to happen and that, whatever it was, it would not be good. *How long will it be before our luck runs out? Things change fast at the bottom of the world, and Nature, as unrelenting and deceitful as She was, had yet to show anything but indifference to their needs, much less their very existence.*

Maybe this feeling will be gone in the morning.

The next morning, at 5:00 AM, Captain Muñoz sent a launch for Grant and Ted. Once they were aboard, the *Lientur* set a course south from Base O'Higgins toward 64 degrees south latitude. The captain took no issue with any of Grant's recommendations regarding landing zones *except for one*, an area long known for instability in the Continental Glacier, with a high probability of calving during the austral summer.

By 11:00 AM, the *Lientur* was standing one-quarter mile off the first site identified on Grant's map. As the ship continued to maneuver to avoid icebergs in the channel, Captain Muñoz issued orders to his crew.

"CWO Lucero, prepare un bote con tripulación para ayudar a los dos científicos."[155]

"Si, Capitán!"

It took fifteen minutes for the *Lientur's* crew to place a motorized launch in the water. Once there, the helmsman, motorman, and two additional seamen, together with Grant and Ted, climbed down a rope ladder and took their positions. With everything ready, the motorman started the engine, and the helmsman set course for the beach.

The surf was low, and it was relatively easy for the crew to land and offload the two scientists and their equipment before they backed the launch out, away from the surf and ice floating near the shore that could damage the boat. An additional threat at this time of year, too, was the constant calving of the Continental Glacier, as the thawing of the ice caused those portions of the glacier nearest to the sea to break off and fall into the water. If the launch stayed near shore, and if the glacier calved while it was there, the possibility of the boat being destroyed, with a total loss of life, was high.[156] [157]

---

155 "CWO Lucero, prepare a launch and crew to support a landing party of two scientists."

156 http://www.youtube.com/watch?v=HbUIRELqowg The boaters in this clip were lucky!

157 http://www.youtube.com/watch?v=U-oo1WqgKe4&feature=related This film shows a wave created by calving of the Continental Glacier that hit a large ship moving near the shore.

The crew took the launch 200 feet seaward to wait for the team's return. If everything went as planned, the field work would take an hour.

Grant and Ted tromped slowly up the glacier through a smooth, narrow depression that sloped down to the beach at this location. Using picks and climbing boots, they finally reached the top. From there, they walked inland 1000 feet to the sought-after outcrop.

Grant chipped rock samples from various strata in the outcrop, stopping occasionally to ask Ted to photograph the strata using his pick to show scale. Ted also bagged and tagged the samples for shipment back to Madison for analysis while Grant recorded preliminary observations in a field notebook.

The outcrop, which comprised sedimentary rocks, was complex. The men became increasingly engrossed analyzing the various layers, each representing a different period in geologic time.

Grant had just finished making a note in his log when a shot rang out and reverberated across the ice! Then another! Two sharp *cracks* that could not have come from anything but a rifle. In short order, two more shots followed. The men threw themselves to the ground and hugged the ice.

For a moment, the air was still. Then, Grant and Ted watched in horror and disbelief as great chunks of snow and ice at distances of 500 feet and beyond to their left and right slowly started to move toward the sea. Great crevasses opened with thunderous *cracks*, making it sound as if the area were being struck repeatedly by lightning. The Continental Glacier was calving before their eyes, with ice masses below where they were standing breaking off and falling into the sea.

"Let's get the hell out of here!" Grant shouted as he and Ted dumped everything into their canvas field bags, slung them over their shoulders, and raced down the hill toward the ocean, occasionally tripping and tumbling head over heels until they could regain their footing and continue as fast as their legs and the snow-covered ice would allow them to run.

When they reached the beach, it was being washed by 5-foot ice-laden waves. They saw immediately what had happened. On a piece of ice, now fifty feet off the beach, lay three dead seals, blood streaming from head wounds inflicted by rifle shots.

Ted recalled hearing the men at the base asking several sailors to shoot some seals, if possible, because the supply of dog meat at O'Higgins was running dangerously low. Obviously, the sailors in the launch had seen the seals surface and move onto the ice. Mindful of the shortage of dog meat, they shot the seals *without thinking of the consequences*. Now, they had triggered a series of major avalanches on either side of the beach on which they had landed just thirty minutes earlier, flooding the area with turbulent, ice-laden water.

Grant and Ted stood back as far as they could and waved their arms to attract the attention of the helmsman. Fortunately, he saw them immediately and, working with the motorman, made a dash for the beach, almost capsizing at one point. The launch rammed into the pebbly beach and came to a grinding halt, buffeted on both sides by the agitated surf and floating ice. A passing swell lifted the boat for a moment. The motorman pushed the throttle forward, sending the launch up the beach a little farther and within reach of Grant and Ted, who threw their bags in and jumped into the boat.

On the next swell, the motorman reversed the throttle, and the launch lurched out as quickly as it had come in. The helmsman took it back 100 feet before turning around and running ahead of a giant wave that had just been unleashed by the thunderous collapse of the calving glacier. If they had delayed even two seconds more, the boat would have capsized, and there would have been nothing any of them could have done to save their lives.[158]

Damn them, thought Ted. *That was close. And for what? Three lousy seals? They could have gotten us all killed. Who the hell is going to pay for* that *stupidity?*

He need not have worried about that. Someone, namely the *Lientur's* captain, would attend to that matter. He had seen it all through his binoculars. After receiving a radio message from Base Prat that storms were headed their way, the captain issued an order to the bridge, "Take the *Lientur* toward shore and prepare to recover the launch."

The captain was fully aware of those responsible for the debacle. *I will reduce the ranks of the two seamen who shot the seals by two pay grades. They should count themselves lucky I don't court martial them,* he thought. *But then,* I *would have some explaining to do as well. God have mercy on me . . . these gringos are going to be the death of me yet!*

By the time the launch returned to the *Lientur*, the sky was darkening. In the twenty minutes it took to retrieve the men and the launch, it turned pitch black, and the wind increased to more than forty miles per hour.

When everyone was safely aboard, the captain met with Grant and Ted in his cabin. He poured each of them a glass of

158 http://www.youtube.com/watch?v=SGsQdF2fELo&feature=related

Scotch and toasted their health. *"Salud!"* Then, riveting Grant and Stone to their seats with his eyes, the captain asked, "How many lives do you think you have?"

"I beg your pardon?" The captain's question caught Grant off guard.

"Señor, you and the English have a saying, something about a cat having nine lives.[159] I don't know how many you have been given, but based on what I've seen and heard, you and Señor Stone appear to be using yours up unusually fast. May I respectfully ask, as your captain, that you be especially careful as to what you do in the future *anywhere in the Chilean Antarctic, and especially so at those times when* I *am responsible for you?"*

As he spoke, the intensity of his voice rose. He was polite, but it was clear that what he said was more of an order than a request.

"It's one thing for us to lose one of our own down here," continued the captain, calming down some, "something that has consequences far beyond anything you can ever imagine. The Comodoro, the Commandante of Base O'Higgins, and I still must face several Army and Navy Boards of Inquiry in Santiago when the Expedition returns in March because of what happened to Sergeant Rodríguez. Believe me, those will *not* be pleasant!"

His voice began to rise again. "And I most certainly do *not* want to be the one who must explain to your Ambassador to Chile how *our* great Navy managed to lose two University of Wisconsin scientists who were performing work in *our* national

---

159 "Good king of cats, nothing but one of your nine lives," William Shakespeare, Romeo and Juliet, Act III, Scene I, Line 51

Antarctic territory under the sponsorship of *our* federal government! *Do you understand?"*

All Grant and Ted could do was nod. There were no words they could utter under these circumstances that would placate the captain. Only actions would suffice now.

"Good! Then we understand each other," said the captain, with an air of certainty that his message had gotten through to Grant and Ted.

"From now on, work as quickly as possible. Go in, get what you need, get out! I don't want you out of my sight any longer than is absolutely necessary. If we can work under those rules, everything will be fine! I won't rest easy until I deliver you back to the *Piloto Pardo* for the voyage north!"

By now the ship had turned into the storm and set course for Base Prat in the South Shetlands. Work on the Antarctic Peninsula would have to wait for another day. For now, the only thing on Captain Muñoz's mind was bringing his ship, crew, and passengers safely through the mounting storm.

XI
In Death's Grip

The *Lientur* left Base Prat[160] on Greenwich Island, South Shetlands, around 10:00 PM, February 18th, heading back across the Bransfield Strait toward the Antarctic Peninsula. Around 6:00 AM, the ship slowed to a crawl just off the Peninsula, maintaining some degree of maneuverability to avoid icebergs.

"CWO Lucero, prepare un bote con tripulación para ayudar a los dos científicos."[161]

"Si, Capitán!"

"Captain Muñoz! Sir!" It was Commander Barbudo. "Request permission to accompany the shore party."

"Any particular reason, commander?"

"Sir, I haven't spent any time ashore in weeks, and I'd like to stretch my legs. Also, I haven't had a chance to take many pictures on the continent with my new 35mm single-lens reflex camera, and this would be a great opportunity to do that."

"Very well. Permission granted. While you're at it, keep an eye on the gringos!" he said, spitting contemptuously over the railing. "They're nothing but trouble!"

---

160 Named for Agustín Arturo Prat Chacón, a Chilean naval officer. See, for example, http://en.wikipedia.org/wiki/Arturo_Prat

161 "CWO Lucero, prepare a launch and crew to support a landing party of two scientists."

Lucero had been standing next to the captain during this exchange. His eyes narrowed as he took in the conversation between the captain and Commander Barbudo. This was the opportunity for which he and Bellolio had been waiting! He licked his licks as he contemplated his next move. He issued an order.

"CPO Bellolio, prepare un bote con tripulación para ayudar en la expedición a tres personas.[162] *Tú estás a cargo y desembarcarás con ellos."*[163]

"Si, CWO Lucero!"

The crew put down a motorized launch, and the field party set off. On the boat were four enlisted men, including Chief Petty Officer Bellolio, who was the senior enlisted man, in addition to Commander Barbudo, Grant, and Ted.

The crew put down a motorized launch, and the field party set off.[164]

162 "CPO Bellolio, prepare a launch and crew to support a landing party of three persons."

163 "You are in charge and will go ashore with the landing party."

164 Photo by BigStockPhoto

Ted was happy that Cristian decided to come with them; he and the commander always found something interesting to discuss.

The landing party had been at sea for ten minutes when clouds and fog rolled in, engulfing them in a blinding snowstorm. They pushed on for twenty more minutes before reaching the area of interest. By now, everyone was cold, and their parkas were covered with snow and ice.

It reminded Ted of what he had read about Shackleton and his men during their voyage on the lifeboat, the *James Caird,*[165] [166] how snow, sleet, and rain had frozen to their eyebrows, mustaches, and beards, giving their faces a ghastly appearance and making even the slightest facial movement painful. If the storm did not break, did he and the others in the launch face this and even greater challenges as they made their way to shore? Captain Muñoz's 'order' to stay out of trouble still rang in his ears.

As luck would have it, the sky slowly cleared, the air warmed a little, and once again, Grant's and Ted's hopes were raised that today, finally, they might be able to accomplish what they had planned to do weeks earlier.

Unfortunately, the sea still was rough, and despite the expert skills of the Navy crewmen, there simply was no way to land at the preferred site. Bellolio looked at his map, glanced at the shoreline, then directed his men to take the launch to the south a few hundred yards, where, despite the heavy surf, he ordered them to take the boat in.

The landing was accomplished with a minimum of trouble, and once the boat had bottomed on the pebbly beach, Bellolio,

---

165 http://www.antarcticconnection.com/antarctic/shackleton/caird.shtml

166 http://en.wikipedia.org/wiki/Voyage_of_the_James_Caird

Barbudo, Grant, and Ted jumped ashore. The remaining three men then took the launch back into the bay so that it would not be dashed to splinters on the rocks while they waited for the field team's return.

The field party of four now picked their way carefully up the edge of the Continental Glacier and made their way inland about a quarter of a mile. They moved carefully among the many deep crevasses, using long, loose ropes to tie themselves together. Only two men moved at a time while the others remained stationary, their ends of the lines tied to stakes driven into the ice. If someone fell into a crevasse, at least their fall would be stopped and their rescue initiated by means of these safety ropes.

The team soon reached the outcrop, and Grant began mapping the area. With that accomplished, he and Ted began collecting and bagging small rock and fossil samples for shipment back to the University of Wisconsin.

While Bellolio walked around and simply took in the scenery, Barbudo set up his tripod, took his camera out from under his left armpit—where the air was sufficiently warm so that the mechanism and film did not freeze—set the camera on the tripod, and snapped pictures he intended to have framed for mounting on his living room walls. Ted was in awe; from their height above the water, he reveled in the panoramic scene that lay before him. It was magnificent. *Few, indeed, were the people who would ever experience anything like this!*

He opened the canvas bag containing the University's small, War-surplus high-frequency transceiver, turned the set on, gave it time to warm up, and tuned it to the agreed-upon call frequency in one of the maritime radio bands. Before leaving, the team had agreed to check in with the *Lientur's* radio operator every thirty minutes, and it was time to meet that schedule.

The antenna, as usual, was a simple insulated wire sixty feet long that Ted let out onto the snow, and the transmitter loaded easily at 6300 kHz. The *Lientur* was maneuvering two or three nautical miles offshore, so contact was established immediately. Having assured the captain that all was well in the field, the work proceeded for several hours, with the team stopping only to eat and Ted making radio contact every thirty minutes. The launch and its crew waited offshore.

The radio check at 3:00 PM yielded bad news from the *Lientur*. Another storm was fast approaching, and Captain Muñoz ordered the field team back to the ship immediately. Ted packed up the radio while Bellolio and Barbudo helped Grant pack his samples into a makeshift canvas 'sled' that they would use to drag the rock and fossil samples down the glacier. By now, the sky had started to darken, and the wind was picking up. When all was ready, the team began their descent, with Bellolio leading the way down the glacier, followed by Grant, Ted, and Barbudo, who turned around every once in a while to snap still another picture.

The distance between each person was thirty feet, with sufficient slack in the ropes between them to provide a measure of safety in the event someone fell either onto the glacier's surface *or into a crevasse*. As was the case on the way up, the men in positions 1 and 3 moved forward twenty steps at a time, planted an ice pick deep into the ice, and waited for the men in positions 2 and 4 to move up twenty steps. They had gone

300 yards down the glacier in this manner when they heard a thunderous roar.

The ice beneath their feet shifted seaward by ten feet, knocking the entire party to the ground. The tension on the rope linking Ted to Barbudo was cutting into Ted's waist, making it almost unbearable to move. Jerking himself around, Ted anxiously looked back up the glacier. The commander was gone! Vanished! He had fallen into the crevasse that had opened up. *If he's still alive,* thought Ted, *he's hanging at the end of this rope!*

The men called out to Cristian, but given the wind and the distances involved, they had no way of knowing if he heard them. Nor did they hear Barbudo calling to them.

Embedding the heels of his boots into the ice and snow, Ted quickly drove his ice pick deep into the ice to his left and, mustering every bit of strength left in his body, eased the rope attached to Barbudo around the handle until he was able to release some of the strain on his waist. With that done, he used his geology pick to drive two stakes into the ice near the ice pick and wound the rope around all three implements. Then, he untied the rope tethered to Barbudo from his body.

"Grant, Bellolio," shouted Ted, "come up here. I need you to tie a rope to my waist and help me if I get into trouble. I'm going back for the commander."

Grant and Bellolio began moving up the glacier, this time being even more careful lest other crevasses or a snow bridge[167] open in their path. They could hear the ice cracking, with minor movements of the surface a constant reminder of the glacier's instability.

[167] A snow bridge is an arc across a crevasse.

"Pound another pick and more stakes into the ground here," Grant shouted. "They'll serve as good anchors for Ted." Working quickly, the three men pounded an ice pick and two more stakes into the glacier's surface ice, and gave one end of a fifty-foot nylon rope four turns around them. They tied the other end around Ted's waist.

"I think we're ready, Ted. We'll let the line out slowly. Just let us know if you need anything," said Grant as he and Bellolio slowly started to let out the line.

Ted crawled on his stomach to the edge of the crevasse, spreading his body across the ice to the maximum extent possible to distribute his weight over the surface. When he reached the edge of the crevasse, he peered over the edge. Roughly twenty feet below the glacier's surface lay Barbudo, his right arm bent awkwardly under his body, blood streaming from under his body from a serious wound. "Cristian! Can you hear me?"

No response. "Cristian! Cristian!"

Motioning that he was going to rappel down the side of the crevasse to the ledge where Barbudo had fallen, Ted turned, put his feet over the edge, and started to let himself down. Another thunderous roar broke the silence! The crevasse opened further, now some twenty feet across, with a depth of hundreds of feet.

The jolt dislodged the ice picks and stakes holding Ted's and Barbudo's lifelines, burning Grant's and Bellolio's hands despite the gloves they were wearing, and slowing but not preventing Ted and Barbudo from falling to a second ice ledge, this one thirty feet below the glacier's surface. Fortunately, the line around Ted's waist broke his fall, but still, he hit the ice hard, landing on his right foot before toppling onto the ledge.

There they both lay, Barbudo, unconscious, and Ted, going in and out of consciousness. What was left of their nylon ropes hung in shreds, cut by the ice and left above, on, and below the ledge and northern wall of the crevasse.

"Help me, señor, please!" Bellolio shouted to Grant. "I must see where they are."

Together, Bellolio and Morris drove an ice pick and two stakes into the ice and soon had tied a secure lifeline tied around Bellolio's waist.

Now Bellolio crawled on his stomach slowly up the glacier to the edge of the crevasse. He peered down and saw the two bodies. *They may be alive,* he thought, *but I'm not going to risk my life for the likes of Barbudo, given the threat he poses to me and Lucero! Besides, while not exactly the kind of* accidente *Raul had in mind, this will do. What we need now is time for them to die. If they're not already dead, and if we're lucky, the weather will move in and there will be no possibility of anyone retrieving their bodies.*

Backing down the glacier on his stomach to where Grant sat waiting, Bellolio delivered the tragic news: "*Señor, lo siento mucho.* I am so sorry. I think they are dead. There is nothing we can do for them. Even now, another break in the ice could trap or kill us. We must return to the *Lientur.* Captain Muñoz will know what to do. Unfortunately, we can not radio for help because the radio is in the crevasse with Señor Stone."

Grant was anguished. He wrung his hands over and over. "There must be something we can do!" he kept repeating. "We must do *something!*" He put on his crampons and started moving up the glacier, toward the crevasse. Bellolio grabbed his arm and pulled him back.

"No, señor! There's nothing we can do! We must leave before we are trapped, too. Believe me, we must go now, or we will die!"

Grant looked sick to his stomach. He and Bellolio quickly coiled the unused ropes and descended as quickly as they could to the beach.

The launch was waiting for them. The helmsman had brought it in when the radio operator aboard the *Lientur* asked why the team had not begun their return to the ship. Based on what Bellolio told him, the helmsman now radioed the ship, adding that Morris and Bellolio would brief the captain as soon as they were aboard.

The storm engulfed the entire area within a matter of minutes, bringing its full fury to bear on the launch and its passengers. Slowly they made their way seaward, toward the *Lientur*. Within minutes, Morris, Bellolio, and the crew were soaked. By the time the launch reached the ship, one-half mile from shore, the sea, roiled by forty mile per hour winds, had waves topping fifteen feet. Recovery of the personnel, crew, and the launch took more than thirty minutes.

"¿Qué pasó?"[168] Lucero hissed through his teeth as Bellolio passed him on his way back to his quarters. Bellolio was soaked to his skin. Salt water dripped from his hair, face and clothing, leaving pools on the deck. Despite being wrapped in a heavy woolen blanket, he was shivering so badly that he could barely speak.

168 "What happened?"

"¡Por Dios santo, me estoy muriendo de frío. Dejáme al menos cambiarme la ropa, Raul!"[169]

Bellolio stripped and headed toward the shower. Standing there under a stream of hot water and drinking from a bottle of cheap whisky Lucero had handed him, he quickly related what happened.

"I'm sorry Stone got in the way," said Lucero, pursing his lips, "but Barbudo was a real threat to us! We had to do something. A few more weeks, perhaps even days, and we could have ended up in the brig. Are you sure they're both dead?"

"Well," said Bellolio, hedging a bit as he shut the water off and reached for a towel, "no, I'm not sure."

"What?" yelled Lucero, before catching himself and repeating what he had said in a coarse whisper. "What?"

"I couldn't see real well down the crevasse, Raul. They was down twenty to thirty feet, lying on a ledge. The commander's injuries looked serious. He looked to be bleeding real bad. Stone was on his right. He didn't appear to be in as bad shape as the commander. But neither of them was movin', I can tell you that. I carefully let loose the last line that was entangled around an ice pick that was stuck in the ice at the top of the crevasse. The other gringo didn't see me do it. I let everything slip nice and slowly into the crevasse. If they're still alive, they won't be able to climb out, even if they had the strength!"

"That's good, Eduardo, that's good." Lucero made a fist and kneaded it into the palm of his other hand. He looked like he wanted to punch Eduardo. "Now, what the hell did you tell the captain when you got back on deck?"

---

169 "For God's sake, I'm freezing to death. Let me at least change my clothes, Raul!"

"I told him that I thought they was dead, that the fall had killed them, and that there was no way for us to rescue them without endangering our lives. With a storm brewing and no place to anchor, I was sure the captain would take the ship back to Prat. By the time he returned, they'd be dead for sure."

"Okay, okay. Well, we better hope that happens, my friend. Otherwise, the captain could send a launch back as early as tomorrow morning. If one or both of them are alive and they saw you drop the lines, *you* are going to have to answer some embarrassing questions!"

Just then, Petty Officer Pedro Barriga walked into the shower room. "You had a close call, Eduardo. I'm sorry about Barbudo and the gringo, but happy to see that you made it back alive."

"Thanks, Pedro. I wasn't sure I'd ever see the *Lientur* again, what with the way those crevasses opened up, and how the storm blew up so fast."

Barriga picked up the bar of soap he had forgotten earlier that day and left the room. Lucero turned back to Bellolio.

"*If* they survived," hissed Lucero through clenched teeth, "and *if* the captain waits out the storm and sends a boat ashore in the next 24 hours, then they *both* pose a threat to us. Even if the commander is dead and Stone survived, we could have a problem. What if the commander told Stone everything he knows before he died? We ain't free and clear yet, Eduardo!"

Muñoz picked up the handset on his phone and dialed the radio room. "Commander, get me the captain of the *Pardo*."

"Yes, sir. It may take a few minutes. I need to get their attention on the calling frequency, then move them higher in the band, where the atmospheric noise is lower."

"Commander, I need a secure link, and I need it *now!*"

"Yes, sir."

Fulfilling the captain's order would not be easy. It was late on a summer afternoon in the southern hemisphere and the sun was beginning its descent. The 220-nautical-mile distance between the *Lientur,* under way off the North Antarctic Peninsula, and the *Piloto Pardo,* maneuvering off the old British Antarctic Survey base on Anvers Island,[170] meant that communications would have to be conducted in the *lower portion of the shortwave band.*

Unfortunately, atmospheric noise in this portion of the radio spectrum was at its seasonal high. Thunderstorm activity was raging over South America, Africa, Southeast Asia, and Australia. Energy released by thousands of lightning strikes across the globe *every second* was propagating through the ionosphere just as would radio signals, except that the 'signals' from the lightning strikes now were beginning to blanket the entire lower portion of the shortwave band.

This was not a case of an occasional static burst obliterating a word or two of a broadcast. Under the conditions that prevailed, whole sentences could get swallowed up. Adding to the problem was a constant 'rushing' sound in the receiver's audio output caused by 'snow static.'[171]

---

170 http://en.wikipedia.org/wiki/Anvers_Island

171 Snowflakes pick up a charge as they fall and deposit it on an antenna when the strike that conductor, causing a constant 'rushing' sound. To hear the effect heard in a receiver, listen to: http://www.audiosparx.com/sa/archive/default/default/Radio-static-buzz-close-up-constant-only-snow-no-voice/202456

It would take an experienced radio operator to find the 'sweet spot' in the lower portion of the radio spectrum—not too high in frequency, not too low, with a minimum of noise—to initiate communications over the path between the two ships.

Fortunately for the captain, the *Lientur's* duty radio officer, Lieutenant-Commander Ricardo Santibañez, had more than ten years of experience with high-frequency[172] communications, including three years of experience on expeditions to the Antarctic.

It took Commander Santibañez 10 minutes to contact the *Piloto Pardo* and move their operator to a less noisy frequency in a dedicated marine band. "I have the Captain on a secure link, sir."

"Sir, this is Capitán Muñoz. I have a problem. Can you hear me? Over."

"Yes, Muñoz. I can hearϟϟϟwithϟϟϟϟϟϟculty. ϟϟϟϟϟϟϟ static. Over."

"Sir, two men have fallen into a crevasse, about 300 meters inland . . . an American scientist, Stone, and my man, Commander Barbudo. Over."

"Stand by, Muñoz . . . IϟϟϟϟnotifyϟϟϟThe commodore."

Minutes passed.

"Muñoz, thisϟϟϟel Comodoro don Marceloϟϟϟϟϟϟϟϟϟ Altamirano.[173] Over."

Muñoz immediately reviewed with the admiral what he had told the captain of the *Piloto Pardo*, repeating several key points on two occasions when signal fading and static obliterated his

---

172 The high-frequency, or HF, band extends from 3.0 to 30.0 MHz. It sometimes is referred to as the 'shortwave' band.

173 The Commodore is a Rear Admiral

signal at the other end of the link. When he finished the last of several transmissions and turned the exchange over to the commodore, all he heard was static.

Then, he heard the commodore's voice burst through the noise.

"Muñoz! What the HellϟϟϟϟϟϟdoingϟThere? This Expedition already lost one Army non-ϟϟϟϟϟ officer and,ϟϟϟ because of that, we have to faceϟϟϟϟϟϟwhen we get backϟϟϟ ϟϟϟϟϟSantiago. Now, you lost one Americanϟϟϟϟϟandϟϟϟϟ ϟϟϟϟϟ. How did you let this ϟϟϟϟϟϟ? Dammit, ϟϟϟϟϟϟϟϟϟ ϟϟϟ doing about it? Over!"

"Sir, I take full responsibility. I validated the landing site using their and our maps, instructed the Americans to work quickly, and sent Commander Barbudo and CPO Bellolio with them to ensure their safety. I would have gone myself if it would have prevented this. We're in the middle of a bad storm. I moved to sea to avoid the ice. I must see if this storm will abate before I can determine whether I can go ashore or must set course for Prat. My first obligation is to my ship and my men! Over."

"Muñoz! I didn't say that youϟϟϟϟϟϟthe *blame*! I saidϟϟϟϟϟϟI'm *blaming* you! Dammit, if you don'tϟϟϟleast recover the bodies, and ϟϟϟϟcially the American's, you and I will be drummed outϟϟϟϟϟϟservice . . . and I'm supposed toϟϟϟappearϟϟϟϟPromotion Board forϟϟϟmotion to Vice Admiral next August! ϟϟϟϟϟϟϟϟϟϟϟ understand me? Take action, Muñoz! If you don't bringϟϟϟϟto an early conclusion, I'm goingϟϟϟbust you so low in rankϟϟϟϟϟϟwill wish youϟϟϟϟϟϟback picking up rocks inϟϟϟϟϟϟcopper mine. Out!

Muñoz looked at the handset in stunned silence. It took him a moment to get his bearings. *The admiral was correct,* he thought; *the action is mine to take. I have to do something, and I have to do it soon. Based on what Bellolio said, there still may be a chance that Barbudo and Stone are alive. Do I stay here and ride out the storm or head for Prat?*

The captain now faced the most difficult command decision he ever had to make in his entire career: move farther to sea, wait out the storm—there better to avoid the many icebergs that were being pushed northward by the wind—then, move back toward shore for the purpose of sending in a team to rescue the commander and Stone, *or* set course for a safe harbor at Greenwich Island, returning in a few days to recover their bodies.

He knew that any decision to send a rescue team to the Peninsula now could later be viewed by his superiors as an exercise in bad judgment, given that it could result in the loss of additional lives. Dare he chance it? The well-being of his ship and many lives hung in the balance.

The *Lientur* moved on through the storm, the tips of her radio masts glowing with St. Elmo's fire.[174] Muñoz took to the bridge, there better to guide his vessel through the increasingly turbulent seas populated by towering icebergs that loomed out of the driving snow and passed to their port and starboard like ghosts in the night.

Except for Munoz's orders to the helmsman, the bridge was silent.

---

174 An electrical weather phenomenon in which luminous plasma is created by a coronal discharge originating from a grounded object in an atmospheric electric field. See, for example, http://en.wikipedia.org/wiki/St._Elmo's_fire

It was 9:00 PM when Ted woke up. The wind was dying, and the sky was clearing. Heavy black clouds swept by overhead, pushed by the strong winds at the higher altitudes. Slowly, the clouds thinned, and sunlight once again bathed the area. Though the sun was low in the sky at this hour, he could clearly see around him. A sharp, throbbing pain in his left leg brought his hand to his torn left pants leg, which felt warm and wet. When he pulled his hand away, it was covered with blood.

He remembered what Rolf Bjornstad had told them at the seminar in at the lodge on the Blue Ridge Parkway: *Use your head to save your ass!* Ripping away the fabric around the wound, he found a 6-inch gash, the skin having been cut by the jagged ice as he fell over the side of the crevasse. *Use your head!* he thought as he quickly pulled antiseptic wipes from his first aid kit and cleansed the wound. *Use your head!* He applied some antibiotic ointment and a large pressure bandage. The survival and medical training they received in the Blue Ridge Mountains that previous October was paying off.

He looked around, and in the dim light some five feet to his left he saw Cristian lying on his back, his right arm bent awkwardly behind him. The ledge around him was stained deep red, a sign, Ted knew, that he was bleeding profusely. If Ted did not get to him soon and stop the bleeding, he would die from either loss of blood or hypothermia.

Inside the crevasse, the sound of cracking ice was deafening. It was as if he were caught in the middle of a Wisconsin cornfield during an afternoon thunderstorm.[175] Ted tried to stand, but instantly realized that he had sprained his right ankle in the

---

175 http://www.therecordist.com/pages/downloads.html Listen to the file entitled AvalanchSnowCrack_AVA_038

fall. His only recourse was to drag himself, inch by inch, along the ice ledge to where Cristian lay. When he finally reached him, he gently nudged the commander's shoulder.

"Cristian, can you hear me? Wake up."

Ted carefully nudged Cristian's shoulder again, and the pain apparently caused him to stir. He opened his eyes. "*Teodoro, mi amigo?* Where are we? What happened?"

Ted explained how Cristian had fallen into a crevasse and broken his arm, which was bleeding profusely, and how when he, Ted, had tried to rescue him, he had fallen victim to Nature as well.

"*Lo siento mucho, Teodoro.* I am so sorry, my dear friend," Barbudo whispered hoarsely. "You should have left me here and gone on. I don't think I'm going to make it."

He coughed up blood, which told Ted that his injuries were far worse than just to his arm.

Ted reached for his canteen, which he kept next to his body for warmth, and gave him some water. Then, he tried to make his friend as comfortable as possible. Barbudo lost consciousness. *Perhaps it's better he sleep and conserve his energy for when a rescue party arrives*, Ted thought.

But will a rescue party arrive in time to save us? What if we have been given up for dead? After all, the ledge is at least thirty feet beneath the surface. That kind of fall could kill a person. I thought I saw Bellolio peering down on us before I blacked out, but now, I'm not so sure he really was there. Was I hallucinating? For Ted, there were no answers to any of these questions.

Then he remembered the radio! It had been strapped over his shoulder, and while it made for a somewhat hard landing, it at least, from all outward appearances, survived intact. Now, he wondered, *will it work?*

He pulled the canvas bag containing the radio from his back and opened it. Pulling the sixty-foot wire antenna from its pocket, he attached it to the transceiver. With trepidation, he pushed the power button to the *ON* position. Instantly, the dial lamp started to glow, brightening as the set warmed up. *Thank God we fixed this radio when we were at Base Prat,* Ted thought.

Soon he heard the static on their calling frequency. He dropped the antenna wire over the edge of the ledge. *Ice won't interfere with the propagation of the signal,* he thought. *If they're monitoring our calling frequency, they should hear me.*

Barbudo stirred, coughed, twisted his body around slightly, and fell back into a light sleep. In attempting to make himself a bit more comfortable, the commander had moved precariously close to the edge of the ledge. Wedging his left foot into a crack in the ice to gain leverage, Ted gently grabbed Barbudo's parka and pulled him back from the edge. *This isn't good, my friend,* thought Ted; *we need to get you to the* Lientur *fast or you're going to die.*

The microphone that came with the manportable transceiver was an olive-drab model T-17 handheld device with a PTT[176] button on the side. Because he did not know how much reserve still remained in the system's batteries, power conservation was paramount. Thus, Ted decided *not* to use AM voice transmissions, but, rather, to *key* the PTT button and use Morse code. This also would help on the other end of the link *if*

[176] Push-to-talk

the operator picked up on the fact that Ted was sending Morse code and retuned the Lientur's receiver for that mode. Doing so would significantly improve the operator's ability to understand what Ted was sending.

The easiest code group to send would be SOS, he thought.[177] And so, over and over again, he sent the three letters, all run together, in sequence, over and over again, stopping every ten seconds or so to listen for an answer. *Nothing heard.* A quick glance at this watch showed him that it was now approaching 10:10 PM. Their only hope was that Bellolio convinced the captain that there still was a chance to save them *or* . . . *OR* . . . that the *Lientur's* duty radio operator still had their auxiliary receiver tuned to their agreed-upon call frequency. A good operator would keep that receiver tuned to that frequency . . . it should be standard operating procedure.

He tried again. SOS . . . SOS . . . SOS↯↯↯↯↯↯↯↯↯↯↯↯↯↯↯ SOS . . . SOS . . . SOS↯↯↯↯↯↯↯↯↯↯↯

Wait . . . something broke the static. Was that a voice? ↯↯↯↯↯↯↯↯↯↯↯↯↯↯↯↯↯↯↯

SOS . . . SOS . . . SOS ↯↯↯↯↯↯↯↯↯↯↯↯↯↯↯↯ SOS . . . SOS . . . SOS ↯↯↯↯↯↯↯↯↯↯↯ SOS . . . SOS . . . SOS ↯↯↯↯↯↯↯↯↯↯↯↯↯↯↯ ↯↯↯↯↯↯↯↯↯↯↯↯↯↯↯↯↯↯↯↯↯↯↯↯↯↯↯↯↯↯↯↯↯↯↯↯↯↯↯

Nothing. Nothing but static. ↯↯↯↯↯↯↯↯↯↯↯↯↯↯↯↯↯↯↯↯↯ ↯↯↯ ↯↯↯ ↯↯↯

[177] SOS is the commonly used International Morse code distress signal (· · ·———· · ·). It is a prosign; that is, it has no meaning. The signal is sent without spacing between the characters.

It seemed hopeless. The dial lamp was beginning to dim. He knew that in addition to the batteries losing their charge, the cold temperatures were reducing battery activity. Shutting the unit off to conserve energy, he turned his attention to Cristian.

"Cristian, can you hear me?" He shook his friend gently.

The commander opened his eyes. "*Teodoro, mi amigo* . . . I'm dying."

"No," protested Ted. "Hang on . . . we're going make it. I've been sending out an SOS. I'm sure someone heard me. I'm going to try again soon."

"It's all right, Teodoro," he said calmly, "don't worry about me. Take care of yourself." The commander coughed up more blood, which Ted wiped away. He tried to turn his body slightly in an attempt to make himself more comfortable, and once again moved perilously close to the edge of the ledge.

Ted grabbed his parka and pulled him back. "Cristian, I'm going to drive an ice piton into the wall and tie you down for the night!" *What I really need is an ice screw,* he thought, but he had none.

Using the pick that had been entangled in the rope released by Bellolio, he drove his last piton into the ice and lashed the commander to the wall, careful not to injure him further. Other than that one piton, the ropes that still hung off them, the ice pick, and the radio, they had no other survival equipment with them.

"Teodoro . . . I need to tell you something . . . it's important . . . listen to me carefully. I'm an officer in the Office of Internal Affairs, working under cover on this Expedition."

Ted was startled by this revelation. He listened intently.

"In 1960," Cristian continued, "a few days after the Valdivia Earthquake, a large number of safe deposit boxes in the Banco Central de Chile branch in Talcahuano were looted of millions of dollars in U.S. and British currency, negotiable securities, gold coins, and jewelry. I suspect the crime was committed by two non-commissioned officers who were then, and are now, serving on the Lientur . . . under Capitán Muñoz. Whether or not Muñoz was involved in the theft is something I have not been able to determine. But I'm convinced, based on my investigations, that the theft was committed by Chief Warrant Officer Lucero and Chief Petty Officer Bellolio. Other than you, now, and me, no one else knows this."

He coughed and motioned toward Ted's canteen for water. After a few sips, he continued.

"As best I can determine, the items stolen from the bank are hidden on Base O'Higgins in a crate consigned to Army First Sergeant Leonardo Rodríguez. As you know, he's dead. I'm convinced his death was no accident, but I have no proof . . . just a hunch." He continued to tell Ted everything he had been able to learn in the case.

Barbudo also mentioned earlier thefts involving the movement of goods from two Fleet Warehouses to the Chilean black market—thefts that not only may have involved Lucero and one other Navy non-com, but also a Chilean naval officer and powerful businessman known throughout the country.

Incredible, thought Ted, trying to take it all in.

"You must be careful whom you share this information with, Teodoro." By now his voice was almost a whisper. "If you tell the wrong people, your life will be in danger. It's entirely possible that Lucero and Bellolio have killed once. They won't stop there if you pose a threat to them."

Ted felt Cristian's hand; it was cold to the touch. He was losing blood, and his temperature was dropping. The commander did not have long to live.

Removing his parka, Ted took off his insulated vest and spread it across Cristian's shoulders before putting his own parka back on.

The commander smiled at him. "Promise that if I never leave this place, you'll ask the captain to return someday with a priest and pray for me. And please, my friend . . . if you would . . . ask Capitán Muñoz to look after my Maria and my daughters, Daniela and Teresa. *Los amo más que a la vida misma.*[178]

"Now, please say the Lord's Prayer[179] with me." With that, he started to say the Prayer. Ted joined in immediately.

"Our Father, which art in Heaven.

Hallowed be thy Name.

Thy kingdom come. Thy will be done, . . . on earth—"

Cristian's voice faltered, becoming almost inaudible.

"I don't think I can finish it, Teodoro," he whispered. "Please . . . go on."

Ted continued:

" . . . as it is in heaven.

---

178 "I love them more than life itself."

179 The Lord's Prayer, also known as the Our Father or Pater noster, is perhaps the best-known prayer in Christianity. On Easter Sunday 2007 it was estimated that 2 billion Catholic, Protestant, and Eastern Orthodox Christians read, recited, or sang the short prayer in hundreds of languages. Two versions of it occur in the New Testament, one in the Gospel of Matthew 6:9–13 as part of the discourse on ostentation, a section of the Sermon on the Mount, and the other in the Gospel of Luke 11:2–4. See: http://en.wikipedia.org/wiki/Lord's_Prayer

Give us this day our daily bread,

And forgive us our trespasses, as we forgive them that trespass against us.

And lead us not into temptation.

But deliver us from evil.

"Amen"[180]

Ted looked down at Cristian. His eyes were closed, and his breathing was labored. Every so often he would stir, but there was no question he was weakening by the minute. *He's not going to make it through the night,* Ted thought. He, too, was exhausted and fell into a deep sleep. The time was 10:30 PM. Above, the wind had died, and the moon had risen high in the sky. The only sounds heard were thunderous roars from the glacier ripping apart.

Ted awoke with a start. He had been dreaming he was lying on his back at his family's summer home in central Wisconsin on a hot summer afternoon, listening to an approaching thunderstorm, all the while waving flies away from his face. What he actually found in front of his eyes when he opened them was the end of an orange nylon cord that had been lowered from above by a rescue party from the *Lientur.*

Ted looked up to see a Chilean sailor rappelling down the side of the crevasse. The time was 1:00 AM. Captain Muñoz had sent a party back to look for Cristian and him!

But when he looked to his left, Cristian was gone!

Ted looked down, but Cristian was nowhere to be seen. Had he slipped over the edge in his sleep? Had he tried to make

180 Source: St. Andrew Bible Missal, 1962

himself more comfortable, and in the process, fallen off the ledge, causing the piton to be torn from the wall simply because of the weight placed on it?

He must have dropped hundreds of feet below the surface, thought Ted. *He could be entombed for decades, if not centuries, frozen in time until the glacier, moving slowly to the sea, gives up his body to the ocean in one final act of Deliverance.*

It did not take the sailor long to descend to the ledge where Ted was trapped. Strapped to the man's back was a sling that he soon fastened around Ted's body. After giving the signal, Chief Petty Officer Acuña and Leading Rate Delgado, stationed at the top, carefully pulled Ted out of the crevasse and onto the glacier's surface. The sailor was not far behind.

"What happened to Commander Barbudo?" Acuña asked, taking one last look down the crevasse.

"I woke up next to the commander . . . tried to make him comfortable during the night . . . even attempted to tie him securely to the wall with a rope and piton." The words came out of Ted's mouth in bursts, partly because of being out of breath, but also because of the pain he was experiencing from his wounds. "When I woke up, he was gone. He must have moved during the night, dislodging the piton. There was nothing, then, to stop him from falling over the edge. He must have died instantly when he hit the bottom. But there's no way of knowing the depth at which his body might be found."

The rescue party discussed the situation a few minutes while Chief Petty Officer Acuña redid Ted's pressure bandage and wound tape around his right ankle. Leading Rate Delgado took another look over the edge to make sure they had done everything possible before leaving. It was clear, however, that any attempt to descend again into the crevasse would be an invitation to disaster.

The Chilean enlisted men stood silently next to the crevasse for a minute, then, brushing back their parka hoods, made the Sign of the Cross. "In the name of the Father, and of the Son, and of the Holy Spirit. Amen."

They prayed silently. When they finished, they again made the Sign of the Cross, put their hoods back on, and reluctantly, with great sadness, gathered the ropes and other paraphernalia they had brought with them in preparation for their descent to the sea.

The team made their way slowly down the Continental Glacier to the beach, ever mindful that the region was far from stable at this time of year. As they descended the last hundred yards, the rescue launch's helmsman, working with the motorman, both of whom had been keeping their craft positioned offshore to avoid the swells and pack ice, nudged the boat forward, gently beaching it on the smooth rocks. The motorman idled the engine, then jumped out to hold the boat steady while Acuña and Delgado carried Ted aboard, seating him in the middle of the craft. At that point, the motorman, who by now had climbed aboard, reversed the engine. Acuña and Delgado pushed the launch off the rocks and jumped aboard, and the party headed back to the *Lientur*.

The sea was getting rougher by the minute as the winds, which had been gusting to between twenty and thirty miles per hour spiked to forty miles per hour, then, higher! The sky to the west again turned an ominous purplish-black, and the clouds thickened by the minute. Maneuvering through a narrow channel between two large icebergs, the boat was caught in a swell and nearly capsized.

Everyone shifted their positions slightly to keep her upright while the helmsman concentrated on steering the launch away from the nearest iceberg. For what seemed an eternity, it seemed as if the launch were in real trouble and in danger of crashing into the ice. But the helmsman and the motorman, working together, skillfully used the swells to maneuver the launch away from the icebergs and out to sea.

And none too soon! For just as the launch cleared the in-shore ice pack, there was a thunderous roar as the Continental Glacier calved, sending a 50-foot wall of ice sliding into the sea and creating an ice-laden wall of water more than 8-feet high . . . a wall of water that was headed directly for the launch.[181] The launch already was moving near its top speed, and the motorman pressed the throttle to its limit. Meanwhile, it had started to sleet and weather conditions were worsening by the minute.

Acuña made radio contact with the *Lientur*. "There is no way, under these conditions, that the ship can come in to meet you," the radio operator told him. "The sea ice and icebergs present far too great a threat to the ship's safety, especially in these high winds. Your only hope is to come out to sea, perhaps one to two nautical miles, and meet us here."

The helmsman pressed on. Between the sea spray and the sleet, everyone was soaked—and freezing. Waves ten feet high

[181] http://www.youtube.com/watch?v=F7MIc4FKS_4&feature=related This is a good example of what one would experience along the North Antarctic Peninsula during the austral summer.

tossed the launch around as if it were a leaf in a hurricane. The launch no sooner would crest one wave than it would plunge down the backside and through the next wave, taking on gallons of water at a time.

Two sailors manned the handpump, but they and the pump were no match for the conditions. Despite their best efforts, the launch slowly was filling with water. To make matters worse, the sleet had turned to snow, the wind was increasing, the waves grew higher, and the visibility dropped to several hundred yards, conditions that would prevent the lookout on the *Lientur* from spotting the launch in time for Captain Muñoz to maneuver his ship into position for recovery.

With the launch rapidly filling with water, the motorman, in desperation, emptied his reserve fuel supply, and Acuña immediately began using the empty fuel container to bail out the water at his feet.

Just when the situation seemed most dire, Delgado spotted the port lamp on the *Lientur*. They had found her! Almost simultaneously, the *Lientur's* radio operator barked a command, "Bring her amidships and prepare to transfer all but the helmsman and the motorman to our deck!"

As the launch pulled alongside the *Lientur*, it dove through two waves so large that Captain Muñoz later would tell the Commodore and the captain of the *Piloto Pardo*, in private, that he thought he was going to lose the launch and all hands at that point, together with any future he might have had as a naval officer.

The helmsman pressed on. By now, the launch's motor was smoking, but there was nothing that could be done. The motorman raised his arms skyward. *"¡Estamos en las manos de*

Dios! Que él tenga misericordia de nosotros."[182] Any moment the engine could catch fire.

Lines soon were secured to the launch, fore and aft, but problems lay ahead. As the sea rose and fell by twenty feet, the launch, one second, was level with the deck of the *Lientur*, and a few seconds later was below the outlets for the ship's bilge pumps, all working overtime. There was no way to jump from the launch to the deck because the sea was rising and falling too fast. Every time it fell, the bilge pumps poured gallon after gallon of seawater into the small launch, increasing the probability that it soon would sink.

In desperation, the captain signaled to Ted that when the launch next drew even with the deck of the *Lientur*, he should hold his arms above his head. At that point, two seamen would grab his outstretched arms and pull him over the railing.

It worked! In short order, all but the helmsman and the motorman were brought aboard in the same manner, and shortly thereafter, under Capítan Muñoz's direction, the *Lientur's* crew recovered the launch and its two-man crew.

---

182 "We are in God's hands! May He have mercy on us."

XII
Rescued!
But Who Can Be Trusted?

Two seamen, one holding each of Ted's arms, pulled him over the ship's railing. The launch already had fallen away beneath him, and now, some twenty feet below the level of the deck, was once again taking on water, both from the rough seas as well as from the bilge pump outflow. The sleet, driven by winds of sixty miles per hour, attacked exposed flesh with a vengeance, and every pellet felt like a bee's sting.

Once Ted's feet were on the deck and he regained some semblance of balance, the captain threw a blanket over his shoulders, thrust a cup of Scotch toward him—a cup Ted barely could hold because his hands were frozen—directed a seaman to bring Ted to the captain's quarters, and indicated he, the captain, would remain on deck until all of his men and the launch were safely aboard. Ted followed the seaman down the stairs from the deck, which already had iced over.

The captain's quarters, constructed of rich mahogany with extensive cabinets and bookshelves, was warm and lit by one lamp in the corner behind the captain's leather-upholstered chair. Other than the storm outside, the only sounds were the drumming of the ship's engines and the ticking of the ship's gimbal-mounted chronometer. Seconds after they entered, the chronometer struck 5 bells.[183] It was 2:30 AM. Had it not been for the storm, they certainly would have seen the sun high in the sky. The seaman brought Ted a large towel, some dry clothes, and a pair of leather boots. "The captain will be with you soon."

Captain Muñoz entered the cabin fifteen minutes later. "Can I offer you a refill?"

Ted smiled weakly and gratefully accepted the offer. It had been almost nineteen hours since he had left the ship with the landing party. Between his own injury as well as the bone-chilling wind, sleet, and snow, not to mention the traumatic loss of his good friend, Commander Barbudo, he was physically and mentally exhausted.

There was a knock on the cabin door. "I've sent for the corpsman. That should be him." The corpsman, Chief Petty Officer Lopez, wasted no time in cleaning the area around the leg wound with an antiseptic, then, injecting the leg with an anesthetic before stitching the six-inch gash closed and dressing the wound. He also redid the tape around Ted's ankle.

"Here, take three of these every six hours for the next three days to ease the pain. I'll look at your leg and ankle each day, and we'll take the stitches out as soon as the healing process has progressed. But in the meantime, sir, please . . . no strenuous activity. I respectfully ask that you stay in your bunk, read, go to the head, go to the mess, do what you want . . . but please, you need rest and time to heal, so whatever you do, do it on this

183 http://boatingsailing.suite101.com/article.cfm/ship_watches_and_bells

ship." One look from Captain Muñoz told Ted that he had little choice but to comply.

In fact, neither the corpsman nor the captain was going to let Ted too far out of his sight for quite some time. It did not take a genius to have seen the fear in Captain Muñoz's eyes when Ted finally had been lifted over the railing. And Ted could only imagine the tongue-lashing meted out by the Commodore when he heard that they might have lost both an officer of the Chilean Navy and a United States research scientist under his watch. Visions of them both losing their commissions surely must have weighed on their minds!

The corpsman gathered his instruments, cotton swabs, and other paraphernalia, and excused himself.

When it was only the two of them again, Captain Muñoz sat next to Ted, loosened his tie, and heaving a sigh of relief, said, "Tell me what happened . . . what happened to Commander Barbudo? I must know everything!"

Ted told him how they had finished working about a half mile inland and were returning to the ship when a large crevasse opened beneath their feet, and how he and Cristian had fallen about thirty feet to a ledge jutting out of the wall of the crevasse. The captain wanted to know every detail, every word they spoke to each other, everything that happened on the ice.

"What seemed strange," Ted said, "was that at one point, just after it happened and before I could get my bearings, I thought I saw Chief Petty Officer Bellolio looking down on us and smiling. Why would he do that?" asked Ted. "Wasn't he the one who alerted the ship's party to the accident and the reason your men came back to rescue us?"

"No. Bellolio said that you both had fallen into a crevasse. He thought you both were dead. The weather wasn't good, as you know, so I moved out to sea a few miles and delayed sending a search party back for your bodies. If I had known your true condition, I would have taken the risk and launched a rescue party immediately. It was your radio signals, picked up on our auxiliary receiver, that convinced me to send a team back when I did."

The captain slumped in his chair, his face hardened. All of a sudden, he exploded, bringing his fist down on his desk with such force that a heavy metal ashtray in one corner fell to the deck.

Ted could see tears well in his eyes. "Cristian and I have known each other since his Naval Academy days, when I was an instructor there in Naval Intelligence. He asked me to be the best man at his and Maria's wedding. *"¡Dios mío, él fue como un hermano para mí!"*[184]

Ted now faced a dilemma. On one hand, Cristian had revealed a considerable amount of information regarding his undercover mission in the Antarctic—information that had to be conveyed to someone on the Expedition, lest it be lost and the two men responsible for the theft in Talcahuano, and most probably Rodríguez's death, make a clean getaway.

On the other hand, there was just the hint in Cristian's words to the effect that Captain Muñoz himself might be a party to the theft. He was, after all, the one who assigned Lucero and Bellolio to guard the bank where the theft took place. And there still were those unexplained thefts several years earlier from at least two Fleet Warehouses that involved the movement of

---

184 "My God, he was like a brother to me!"

goods into the Chilean black market—thefts in which Lucero and other non-coms as well as at least one officer might have been involved.

But hearing the emotion in the captain's voice, and learning of the relationship between him and Cristian, Ted decided that he had no choice but to tell Muñoz everything Cristian had told him before he died.

"Captain, I need to give you some information revealed to me by Cristian . . . information he said could get me killed if it fell into the wrong hands."

The captain was dumbfounded. "You fear for your life?"

The captain ran his fingers through his hair, trying to comprehend what Ted was saying. Finally he said, "You'll be safe on my ship, I assure you. Please, go on."

"Cristian worked for the Office of Internal Affairs," Ted began, with some trepidation. "For more than a year he's been following Lucero and Bellolio, who he was convinced were responsible for the theft from the Banco Central de Chile in Talcahuano following the earthquake in May of 1960. There was no question in his mind that they were responsible for taking the items missing from the safe deposit boxes, but he hadn't been able to learn until recently how they managed to get it out of the bank or where they hid it.

"The break he'd been waiting for came not long ago when Lucero, Bellolio, and Rodríguez went seal hunting at O'Higgins, but only the first two returned.

"Cristian started looking into their backgrounds and found that Lucero and Rodríguez went way back, to their school days in Arica. Then he started poking around the Expedition's inventory of household goods being shipped from the mainland, through Antarctica, and back to Expedition members' homes That's when he stumbled on a crate that entered the system in Talcahuano in May of 1960 under Rodríguez's name. But Rodríguez was nowhere near Talcahuano at the time. Army records show that he was assigned to a unit stationed in Iquique."

"And putting everything together," continued the captain, finishing the line of reasoning that Ted had laid out, "Cristian concluded that the crate that ostensibly held Rodríguez's household goods probably contained the items stolen from the Banco Central de Chile."

"So, Bellolio's smiling down at us from above after we fell into the crevasse and his failure to convey our true situation to you when he returned to the ship," continued Ted, "strongly suggests that somehow Lucero and Bellolio *knew* that Cristian might be on to them, isn't that correct? And if so, all they were waiting for was an opportunity to kill him to protect their identities *and* the crated refrigerator," concluded Ted. "Our accident was their fortuitous opportunity to kill the one man who could thwart their entire plan and send them before a court martial for the killing of Rodríguez. But how could they have known that he was working under cover?"

"My guess is that someone within the Office of Navy Records was tracking the data searches Barbudo requested in his radio messages," intuited Captain Muñoz, "and had their curiosity aroused. It's even possible that Barbudo's contact within Internal Affairs had his interest piqued by what he was receiving from the commander."

"But Cristian wouldn't have sent those messages in the clear, would he?"

"Of course not," responded Muñoz. "Cristian would have used casual, but nevertheless encrypted, messages intended for his contact in Santiago. And the man in Internal Affairs should have been circumspect when dealing with Navy Records. So, at least we know that the number of people who were aware of his activities should be severely limited.

"The trail starts with his contact in Internal Affairs," Muñoz continued, "the person who handled his encrypted messages containing the data requests and who submitted his data requests to Navy Records. He's the prime suspect.

"But I have to include the possibility that it was a person in Navy Records who tipped them off after seeing what the data inquiries yielded. Lucero and Bellolio may even have cut him in for part of the spoils.

"But how would the person in Navy Records know that it was Barbudo making the inquiries? They needed to learn the identity of the person pursuing them. So I suspect that somehow, they succeeded in compromising someone within Internal Affairs as well. They *had* to have done that. There was no other way for whoever was handling the inquiries in Navy Records to know where the messages were coming from!"

Muñoz stared down at the deck, deep in thought. Ted sat there, saying nothing.

The captain closed his eyes and put his head down in his hands. Except for the drumming of the engine and the sound of the chronometer, the captain's quarters were silent. The ship labored toward the South Shetland Islands through the storm that raged over the Bransfield.

Finally, after more than a minute, he raised his head, turned to Ted, and confessed, "I should have known better than to trust Lucero and Bellolio to guard the bank in Talcahuano. Given the consequences, that undoubtedly was the worst decision I've made in my entire life! I knew that both men had been the subject of naval disciplinary actions over the years. But they always executed their military assignments with speed and accuracy. For them to have robbed the bank, killed Rodríguez, then, caused the death of a naval officer is beyond my comprehension.

"I trusted Lucero and Bellolio; Rodríguez must have trusted Lucero. It's an old story, *amigo mío.*" Be careful of those closest to you because they can do the most damage.

"My guess is, Lucero and Bellolio concluded that if they could stop Cristian here, on the ice, they could stop the investigation, or at least impede it long enough to get away with the theft," continued Muñoz.

"So, why not simply arrest Lucero and Bellolio now, and seize the crate?"

"Good question!" answered the captain. "We could, *but* . . . we must know *who* was involved in Santiago and *who,* specifically, tipped off Lucero and Bellolio. Once we know their identities, we can deal with them *and* put Lucero and Bellolio in the brig."

He continued, "We know where the crate is, we know where Lucero and Bellolio are—they're on *my* ship!—and we need to make sure that they can't get anywhere near you. We have to work on the assumption that they believe Cristian lived long enough to tell you what he knew. But you're correct; that certainly *does* put your life in jeopardy!"

Great, thought Ted. *Join a scientific expedition, travel the world, end up a corpse! It's true. If you want to make God laugh, show him your plans!*

"I understand," said Ted anxiously. "So, what do I do now?"

"Well, you must *not* discuss this with anyone else. There's no way of knowing who else might be involved, especially on this ship.

"And for now, I want you to take the bunk just behind the bridge," said the captain. "I'll assign a trusted enlisted man to be with you at all times. And I'll assign Lucero and Bellolio duties that cause them to be confined to other parts of the ship until we reach Greenwich Island. Once there, I will transfer you to the *Piloto Pardo*; you'll be safe there. I'll deal with Lucero and Bellolio when we get back to Punta Arenas, by which time I'll have learned the final shipping instructions posted for the crate."

"I'm sorry about Cristian," said Ted. "I want you to know that I did everything possible to help him and make him comfortable. I considered him to be my friend as well, and I truly regret that I could not have done more. Please tell his wife that he loved her and the children dearly, and he missed them. He also asked that you do what you can to help them through their grief, and that to the extent possible, you look after them.

"Oh, and he did have one last wish."

"What was that, my friend?" asked the captain.

"That if he died, you return to the area with a priest and pray for him."

"On my solemn oath, I will do that," said Captain Muñoz. "I also will talk with his priest and Maria about holding a Funeral Mass for him when I return to Chile.[185]

---

185 The Funeral Mass, which could be held without the presence of a body, would use a covered catafalque (a decorated bier on which a coffin rests in state during a funeral) surrounded by three candles on each side. The covered catafalque would represent the coffin of the deceased. This was done at times prior to Vatican II (1965).

The captain paused for a minute, took a handkerchief out of his coat pocket, and wiped his eyes. "It is tragic to see one so young, with so much to live for, lose his life. I will do everything I can for him and his family."

The captain rang for his aide, who escorted Ted to his bunk. A senior enlisted man took up a post nearby. Ted noticed that he was wearing a sidearm, something unusual for peacetime service. But Ted did not have much time to dwell on the thought because he no sooner had put his head on the pillow and pulled the blanket up to his head than he fell into a deep sleep.

The entire ship shuddered as the bow hung in the air for several seconds before crashing down into the trough between two large waves and plowing through the second as the *Lientur* fought its way west toward the South Shetland Islands. Three bells sounded; it was 5:30 in the morning.

Ted looked to his right. The guard was gone. *Knowing Grant,* he thought, *he's probably strapped into his bunk below deck, in the cabin we were using before this all happened.*

Ted heard a great commotion coming from somewhere below. He could hear people running, but saw no one. Leaning out of his bunk, he peered into the bridge. All he could see there was the wheelman . . . strapped in his chair! The waves were crashing into the bridge's windows, thirty-five feet above the ship's waterline.

Struggling out of his bunk and making his way to the bridge despite the pain in his leg and ankle, Ted recognized the wheelman as the ship's radio operator, Leading Rate Arturo Torre. On occasion, he and Arturo had operated the *Lientur's* radio system on the ham radio bands in the middle of the night using the callsign CE9AY/MM.[186] Ted asked what the commotion was about below deck.

Torre looked around, then, in a hushed voice, said, "Two men killed each other early this morning. I know nothing more."

Ted was stunned. *Was Captain Muñoz one of them? Were the two men Lucero and Bellolio? And if they were, did Muñoz kill them?*

It did not take long to learn the answer. Ted no sooner had turned around to head for the stairs leading below deck when the captain came up from below, shaking his head.

"They're gone, both of them . . . Lucero and Bellolio. Apparently, they got into a fight. We have no idea what the reason might have been, but they stabbed each other."

Ted was stunned.

"I found them," said the captain. "The morning watch, who was supposed to check in with Lucero before he went on duty, reported to the Officer of the Deck that he couldn't find him. I started searching the ship. When I found him, he was lying forward of the engine room bulkhead near the hull, next to Bellolio, who already was dead. He barely had a pulse. I called for help, but it took several minutes before a crewman arrived. We tried to save Lucero, but he'd lost so much blood that there was nothing we could do." The captain looked distraught.

"Please, come to my quarters," he said.

---

186 http://www.waponline.it/Default.aspx?tabid=139. Scroll down about halfway through this Web page and you will find information on the *Lientur*. Shown, too, is a card confirming a contact between CE9AY/MM and a station in the United States, W5BOS, on February 12, 1962. The card confirming the contact is signed by "Ted – W9VZL", the author and the author's callsign at that time.

In shock from the news, Ted followed the captain to his quarters. Muñoz closed the door behind them. "Well," he said, "now it's just you and me who know what's going on . . . and whoever in Navy Records or Internal Affairs tipped them off to Cristian's investigation. I must radio the *Pardo* regarding these deaths. Of course, there will be official Naval Boards of Inquiry as soon as we reach the South Shetlands.

"But this will work to our advantage," he said, pursing his lips and nodding. He already was thinking about what might happen next. "Once whoever was working on the inside with Lucero and Bellolio—and my guess is that it was Lucero who masterminded the entire affair . . . Bellolio wasn't that bright—we'll see the routing paperwork change on Rodríguez's crate. Whoever makes those changes and shows up to claim the crate is our man, and that should close the case.

"In the meantime, we sit tight and watch. Besides, I know where the crate is, and I know it's under seal. I'll make sure that I have it under surveillance, if not under my total control, for the entire voyage back to Punta Arenas as well as in-country, once it leaves the warehouse in Punta Arenas."

The preliminary Naval Boards of Inquiry on Greenwich Island were brief. Though there were no witnesses to the deaths, there also was no evidence to indicate that they were the result of anything other than the wounds the two men inflicted on each other. What caused the fight was deemed a matter of speculation and something that probably never would be known, according to the official record. A more thorough investigation would have to wait until the Expedition returned to the mainland.

Captain Muñoz and the ship's complement were provisionally cleared of any involvement in the "unfortunate event," which was attributed by the Naval Boards of Inquiry to a personal dispute between the two parties. It was directed that their bodies be returned to Punta Arenas at the end of the Expedition for subsequent burial by their families. Further, their final military status was to be determined by a Navy tribunal that would be held in Santiago later that year.

In the aftermath of the Naval Boards of Inquiry, Captain Muñoz asked Ted to take a walk on the pebbly beach with him, "just to stretch my legs," said the captain.

"I think I've figured out what happened on the *Lientur* a few days ago, when Lucero and Bellolio killed each other. Not that it's going to change anything. But I don't like loose ends, and the only explanation that keeps coming to mind is this: I think Lucero knew that, sooner or later, Bellolio would do or say something that would lead the authorities to them both. Bellolio already had been involved in a serious altercation several years ago that cost him two pay grades. He was a hothead and was known to shoot his mouth off at the slightest provocation. Lucero probably figured that at some point, Bellolio would lose control and blurt out their secret.

"So, I think he decided to get rid of Bellolio. Now, you recall that we were in the midst of a severe storm, and the crew was under severe stress. I mean, we had to tie the wheelman to his chair, and no one even could stand for more than a few seconds.

I couldn't tell the Boards of Inquiry this, but I found several loose straps around some heavy crates just above the place on the lower deck where I found the bodies.

"I think Lucero brought Bellolio below deck on the pretense that they needed to talk. What he really intended, I think, was to kill Bellolio, to use those crates, now free to move, to crush him when the ship was struck by a large wave. Maybe Lucero even was going to use his strength to pull the crates down on Bellolio. I don't know. Unfortunately for Lucero, Bellolio must have figured out what was about to happen and they fought . . . to the death, as it turned out. I tightened the straps while my men removed the bodies."

What? thought Ted. *What's going on here? Why would Muñoz alter the crime scene? And why would he even tell what he had done?*

"I know what you're thinking, Teodoro. The reason I tightened the straps was so that there would be no question as to what occurred down there, other than the simple fact that two enlisted men got into a fight and killed each other. If the official inquiries started to look into other evidence and explanations, then it could disrupt my entire investigation into who in Navy Records or Internal Affairs might be involved. The less people involved at this point, the better! What's happened has happened, and whether or not the straps were loosened does not change anything."

Interesting . . . he said 'my entire investigation.' *Since when has he been involved? Did he just enter the case, or has he, too, been looking into the theft, perhaps unbeknownst to Cristian?*

"Well," said Ted, "at the least, I won't have to be looking over my shoulder for the remainder of the Expedition. I wish you well on finding out who contributed to Cristian's death."

"Thank you. I'll find them . . . believe me, I *will* find them. And when I do, I *will* deal with them." There was a look of steeled determination in his eyes unlike anything Ted ever had seen.

It was early in the morning, well after everyone but the helmsman and the officer of the watch had gone to sleep. Ted's mind was reeling; he could not sleep.

Was I responsible for Lucero's and Bellolio's deaths? And what part, if any, did Captain Muñoz play in their deaths? True, he was visibly shaken when he learned that Bellolio had lied about our condition in the crevasse, which had caused him to delay sending a rescue team to our aid. So, it would not be farfetched to think that he had a score to settle, especially given the relationship between him and Commander Cristian. And he certainly indicated that he would deal harshly with the person or persons in Santiago who were working with Lucero or Bellolio, once he determined who they were.

But then he remembered what Cristian had said to him about the captain regarding the bank theft: '*Whether or not Muñoz was involved in the theft is something I have not been able to determine.*'

What if Muñoz was *involved, and what if the fight between Lucero and Bellolio was a convenient opportunity to kill them both? Once they were out of the way, and once he takes care of the people in Santiago who were working with them, the spoils would be Muñoz's for the taking!*

The question now is, is Muñoz a threat to me? Wasn't he the one, after all, who said, 'It's an old story, amigo mío. Be careful of those closest to you because they can do the most damage.'

And yet, Muñoz also had indicated that he was involved in some kind of 'investigation.' Does this mean that in addition to being the Lientur's captain, he also is working in an investigative capacity? Was he working, perhaps, for the Chilean High Command? He did say that he had taught Naval Intelligence at the Academy, so he must have an intelligence background.

Ted's mind was in overdrive. *It would have been entirely possible both for him and Cristian to be working on the same case and not even know about each other's activities. This would not be the first time that two agencies within the same military service worked in isolation, refused to share information, and worked the same case without even a hint as to what a rival agency might be doing.*

Besides, thought Ted, *the theft* did *occur on the captain's 'watch', so to speak. And no doubt some of the victims were high-ranking Chilean naval officers, given that the city was home to a major Navy port. So it might be expected they would order one of their own to investigate the robbery* without *involving the Navy's formal investigative arm.*

What the hell is going on here?

With Lucero and Bellolio no longer a threat to him, and with the *Piloto Pardo* delayed because of weather, Ted had no choice but to remain on the *Lientur.* Given the situation and the suspicions that still surrounded what part, if any, Muñoz might have played in everything that had happened, Ted stayed close to the upper bunk just aft of the bridge, where he would be highly visible. Grant took up residence in the bunk below him. At the least, there would be safety in numbers.

The ship now needed to make one final call at Base PAC on Deception Island for the purpose of transporting wintering-over supplies to that base from Base Prat and to load men and materials from Base PAC for the voyage home. Thus, on February 22nd, the *Lientur* sailed for Deception Island to await the rest of the flotilla.

A radio message received from the *Yelcho* stated that David had indeed been able to secure the necessary gravity readings at Base GGV and French Cove Sub-Base Yelcho. In fact, because of the *Yelcho's* many voyages up and down the North Antarctic Peninsula, conducted for the purpose of allowing him to gather rock samples at various points along the way, David had repeatedly occupied the gravity stations not only at these two bases, but also at Base O'Higgins as well.

"It'll be my pleasure to return your gravimeter the very moment I see you, my dear colleague," David stated during one brief radio exchange. "And I say in all honesty that the moment can come none too soon!"

Ted's response was equally droll. "On behalf of Dr. George P. Woollard and the entire staff of the Geophysical and Polar Research Center, Mr. Green, we extend our deepest appreciation for your efforts!"

XIII
Return to Civilization

The *Piloto Pardo* and *Yelcho* arrived at Deception Island within four hours of one another on the last day of February. The *Piloto Pardo's* crew had been responsible for transferring all personnel not wintering over at Base O'Higgins to their ship, together with any freight, including personal items such as appliances they had brought with them from South America. Thus, the crate containing the refrigerator belonging to Mrs. Rodríguez already was packed in the ship's hold. The *Yelcho's* crew had been responsible for assisting in the closing of Bases GGV and French Cove Sub-Base Yelcho in preparation for the coming austral winter.

Freight destined for Chile that was not already aboard the *Lientur* now was loaded aboard the *Piloto Pardo.* All of the freight from the three ships would be taken to the Fleet Warehouse in Punta Areas. From there it would be shipped to various destinations throughout Chile, both by land and by sea. All that remained now was for the Air Force personnel and scientists who would be returning to Chile to board the *Piloto Pardo,* which would lead the flotilla north to Base Prat on Greenwich Island.

The flotilla left Deception Island late on March 1st. The trip to Base Prat took longer than expected. A heavy fog had descended on the area, and given the pack ice and icebergs that had appeared as a result of summer warming, the danger of collision was high. Watches were posted on the decks of all three ships, and forward speeds were slowed to less than five knots. From time to time, the sound of ice hitting the reinforced hulls reverberated throughout the ships.

Fortunately, the size of the ice encountered and the slow speeds used prevented damage from occurring. The ships reached their destination late on March 2nd. Because of the icebergs around Greenwich Island, all three vessels continued to maneuver to avoid collisions that might otherwise damage their hulls. It would be two days before men, luggage, and crated freight could once again be moved from the base to the ships standing offshore.

To the very end, Nature stubbornly refused to release her grip on the Expedition. She was, at every turn, the most tenacious, ferocious, *indifferent* adversary imaginable, one that showed no mercy, gave 'no quarter,' and, totally unyielding in Her quest for supremacy, strove solely to exact the ultimate price from Her unfortunate victims.

By March 4th, all was in readiness. With the sounding of their whistles and much fanfare from everyone on deck, the flotilla bid farewell to those who would winter-over on Greenwich Island and set a course northwest for Cape Horn.

The *Piloto Pardo*, Flag Ship of the flotilla, passed Cape Horn at 5:10 PM, March 6th. The Drake Passage was uncommonly quiet, though no one complained. It was as if Nature finally . . . *finally* . . . had released the Expedition from her grip and had given its men and ships permission to take leave of Her domain.

The three ships slid silently up the Beagle Canal toward Puerto Williams,[187] a Chilean naval port located on Isla Navarino. They joined the *Lautaro,* which had reached port three days earlier. Once the flotilla's ships were anchored, several officers went ashore in motorized launches to conduct official Navy business and finalize preparations for the celebration to be held the following day.

The next morning dawned bright and clear. Ted hitched a ride ashore on a motorized launch from the *Piloto Pardo* and limping slightly, walked to the base of a bust of John Williams Wilson, an Irish captain, where he took some gravimeter readings. This established a new gravity station on the South American Continent. Hitching a ride back to the *Piloto Pardo* on an inland tug just leaving Puerto Williams, he quickly stowed the gravimeter, changed clothes, and returned to the port for the picnic that the Navy had planned to celebrate the official end of the Expedition.

The featured event prior to the feast was a *fútbol* contest. Better known as soccer in the United States, the game, as played by the teams from the *Piloto Pardo, Lientur, Yelcho,* and the *Lautaro* was *not* for the faint-hearted, and many sailors were taken off the field and driven to the infirmary for bruises, sprains, and other injuries.

The distraction of the game offered Captain Muñoz one last chance to apprise Ted of the situation regarding the crate containing the spoils from the May, 1960, bank robbery.

---

187 http://en.wikipedia.org/wiki/Puerto_Williams

"Teodoro, this probably will be the last time that we will have an opportunity to talk. I've determined who in Navy Records and Internal Affairs was involved in compromising Cristian's cover. And I know where the crate with the refrigerator is located. It's over there," said the captain, pointing at the *Piloto Pardo*, which was anchored next to his ship. "I checked the ship's manifest, and there's no question that the crate was loaded on the *Piloto Pardo* at O'Higgins. It's destined for Punta Arenas. Once there, it will be transferred to my ship for the final leg of the journey to Arica, with stops at Valparaiso, Antofagasta, Talcahuano, and other cities along the way."

The two men looked at each other and smiled.

Ted shook his head from side to side. "I don't believe it."

"Oh, yes," said the captain. "After Rodríguez's death, Lucero had his contact in Navy Records make changes to the crate's routing. He had it moving about the country for three weeks after it arrives in Punta Arenas. This was intended to buy him and Bellolio enough time to meet the shipment in Arica.

"However, immediately after Lucero's and Bellolio's deaths, and before anyone else knew they had died, I changed the shipping instructions, making it appear as if the instructions came from Lucero, so that the crate, instead of embarking on a three-week journey on its own, would instead be transferred to the *Lientur* in Punta Arenas. Lucero's co-conspirators will think nothing of the change, believing that Lucero had learned the *Lientur* would be headed for Arica when the Expedition ends and that this not only would save time, but also let Lucero keep his eye on the merchandise.

"The new instructions also directed that the refrigerator be *held for pickup* at the Fleet Warehouse in Arica instead of having it delivered directly to Rodríguez's widow upon arrival at the port.

"When the co-conspirators find out that Lucero and Bellolio are dead, *their only recourse will be to present themselves to the widow*, using their Navy identification cards to identify themselves. And I know *exactly* what they'll do when they get there.

"First, they'll extend their condolences on behalf of the Service. Then, they'll tell her that as a courtesy to her, the Navy will take care of all matters pertaining to the delivery and set-up of the refrigerator her late husband had wanted her to have *if . . . IF . . . she will just sign the necessary paperwork they have with them so that the Dock Master will release the refrigerator to them for delivery and setup.* She will, of course, not suspect anything and sign the papers.

"When the Dock Master receives the signed papers from these two Navy personnel and hears their story, they'll expect him to release the crate. They probably even plan to take the old refrigerator out for her, saying they'll be more than happy to dispose of it. My guess is, they'll use it to store the stolen goods and masquerade as two old junk dealers for the purpose of making their getaway!"

"Sounds like they think they have it all figured out, doesn't it!" said Ted. "Except—"

"Except," continued the captain, "they haven't counted on me being there. The *Lientur* indeed is putting in at Arica for post-deployment repairs. Between the weather and the ice, we took quite a beating on this voyage and are scheduled to be in-port for six months. I not only will have the excuse I need for being there, but also the time I need to monitor the status and location of the crate."

Wow! thought Ted. *What began as a bank theft, and a significant one at that, now has claimed three lives and turned into a deadly game of cat and mouse, except the mice aren't even aware of the cat that will be lying in wait for them!*

"This matter will be brought to a close, Teodoro, you can be assured of that."

Captain Muñoz had no sooner finished speaking when the commodore approached, exclaiming how successful the Expedition had been and congratulating the captain on his successful rescue effort weeks earlier under the most difficult of conditions. Unspoken but clear was the acknowledgement that Muñoz undoubtedly had saved the admiral's career, something for which he would be forever grateful.

"Come, the games are over. Once again, the men of the *Piloto Pardo* have triumphed!" gloated the commodore.

"It's time to eat," he exclaimed as he waved Captain Muñoz and Ted to the waiting tables laden with clams, empanadas,[188] [189] lamb roasted on a spit, cooked vegetables, and of course, bottles and bottles of the finest red and white Chilean wines. It was hours before people slowly returned to their ships, no doubt for long and well-earned siestas. They would need the rest. The flotilla was scheduled to leave Puerto Williams at 5:00 AM the next day for Punta Arenas.

---

188 http://en.wikipedia.org/wiki/Empanada

189 http://latinfood.about.com/od/appetizersandsnacks/tp/empanadas.htm

Before the captain returned to his ship, he and Ted met one last time, shook hands, and said good-bye. They exchanged a few words about Cristian and the bravery he exhibited to the very end.

"Please don't forget to look after Cristian's wife and two children. At the least, please make sure that they'll be treated well by the Navy and are not left wanting for anything," asked Ted.

The captain nodded, but said nothing. Ted could tell from the look in his eyes that this was something the captain would do, given his respect and admiration for Cristian. Ted did not need a 'sixth sense' to know that there was a special bond between the two men that transcended whatever their official relationship was in the Service. Knowing that, *even at the unspoken level,* was a great comfort to Ted.

They shook hands one last time and parted forever.

The flotilla departed as scheduled. Once underway, the pace was more leisurely. Ted and the other scientists, from both the University of Chile and the University of Wisconsin, were invited to lunch by the commodore. Joining them were the captain and officers of the *Piloto Pardo.* The lunch began with a prayer by the flotilla's chaplain and a moment of silence in memory of Lieutenant-Commander Cristian Barbudo, who died in the line of duty. *The Chilean Navy may never know what a debt of gratitude it really owes Cristian,* Ted thought as the luncheon began.

There were many toasts on the part of all parties. They began with one made by the Commodore: *"¡Por la Universidad de Wisconsin, por la cooperación y ayuda que le ha brindado a la Universidad de Chile y a esta gran expedición al Antártico!"*[190]

Everyone touched their glasses together and drank to what was, without a doubt, the most successful Antarctic Expedition in the country's history.

Grant then stood, tapped his wine glass with a spoon, and toasted the Government of Chile, the men and women of the Chilean Navy, Army, and Air Force—most specifically, of course, the officers and men of the *Piloto Pardo, Yelcho, Lientur, and Lautaro*—and the University of Chile and its scientists.

David followed, toasting Professor O'Mhaille for his persistence in pursuing a joint cooperative effort with the University of Chile through the U.S. National Science Foundation.

Everyone cheered and emptied their wine glasses!

The Commodore sent his steward out for more wine. When it arrived and everyone's glasses had been refilled, he stood and addressed the scientists from the University of Wisconsin. *"Lamento mucho que el profesor O'Mhaille no pueda estar entre nosotros,"*[191] he said, holding up his glass. *"Considero al profesor como una persona de alta estima, y espero que le hagan saber mi profunda gratitud por todo lo que él ha hecho por acrecentar las relaciones entre Chile y los Estados Unidos."*[192]

---

190 "To the University of Wisconsin, for the cooperative assistance it has supplied to the University of Chile and to this great Expedition to the Antarctic!"

191 "I truly am sorry that Professor O'Mhaille is not able to be with us,"

192 "I hold the professor in the highest regard, and request that you convey to him my deepest appreciation for all he has done to further relations between Chile and the United States."

"¡A su salud!"[193]

Grant and David graciously accepted the Commodore's expressions of appreciation for their major professor and promised to convey them to him immediately upon returning to Madison.

As the luncheon was nearing its end, Ted stood, and raising his glass, exclaimed, *"A Teniente 1° Cristian Osvaldo Barbudo Reyes . . . uno de Chile más fino! Podamos nunca lo olvidamos. ¡Salud!"*[194]

Everyone stood up, touched their glasses together, and in silence, drank to Cristian's memory.

The luncheon ended around 4:00 PM with a final prayer by the flotilla's chaplain for the safe return of the fleet to Punta Arenas.

The ships arrived in Punta Arenas on Friday, March 9th, at 8:00 AM. After taking his final gravimeter readings in the city, Ted dashed to the LAN Chile office to make arrangements for his flight home. Grant and David would stay a few days to ensure that their rock samples and field records were well packed and shipped to the States before they left Punta Arenas

Ted flew directly to Santiago the following day. The next two days were spent addressing last-minute matters pertaining to the University of Chile-University of Wisconsin cooperative research program in Geology and Geophysics, picking up mail that had accumulated from the United States while the UW team was returning from Antarctica, securing an exit visa,

193 "To his health!"

194 "To Lieutenant-Commander Cristian Osvaldo Barbudo Reyes . . . one of Chile's finest! May we never forget him. Cheers!"

confirming his ticket at the Panagra ticket office, and packing his personal and Antarctic clothing and survival equipment for the flight home.

Finally, late on March 12th, he took a taxi to the Santiago airport, arriving at 9:00 PM. There, he took the last set of gravimeter readings he would take in South America, passed through customs, and took his seat in the Panagra waiting room. It was late; he had been up since 6:00 AM. His leg throbbed from the injury he had received three weeks earlier on that ill-fated field trip to the Antarctic Peninsula. The long walk from the airport's custom office to the gate did not help, especially given the need to carry both the gravimeter case and his carry-on luggage.

Ted sat down and stared at the floor for several minutes. He suddenly felt a lot older than his twenty-three years. Gone forever from his mind was the carefree existence he had known as a student in Madison, and with it, his innocence. In its place was a new reality, one cold and harsh, in which a person has little or no control over life . . . a reality in which both Nature *and* Man took life swiftly, violently, and without warning. Survival was all that mattered. In that regard, he counted himself lucky to have escaped from the Frozen Continent alive.

His flight would not leave for another two hours, giving him time to reflect on the Expedition. Regardless of where his thoughts wandered, they always returned to one man, Chilean naval officer Commander Cristian Barbudo. *What more could I have done for him?* Ted thought over and over. He could not stop thinking about the night in the crevasse and how devastated he was when he awoke to find that Cristian had fallen from the ledge. He still could 'hear' in his mind the ice cracking . . . thunderous, ear-splitting sounds that repeatedly shattered the silence of the night and that gave indication of the ice bending, cracking, and finally yielding to the most basic forces of Nature.

Cristian was a good man, thought Ted. *He had a wife and two beautiful children, conducted himself ethically in his personal and military dealings, believed in God and lived his life in righteousness. So, why did this happen to* him*? The risks and dangers he faced were no different than those faced by anyone else on the Expedition . . . even less, given that he hardly ever set foot on land.*

Ted sat there for a long time, staring out on the runways. Additional passengers now had come into the waiting room and took seats near the window, watching the runways as well.

As a scientist, he often wondered if it might be possible to interpret good and evil as different representations of two more basic physical properties, order and disorder. He knew that without intervention, anything—a car, house, even a human being—deteriorates and declines with time. So, life, at its most basic level, could be interpreted as the pursuit of order. After all, what would be the worth of living in a world where the order of things increased with time or where order remained constant? *What would we* do *with our time? What would we* do *with our lives?*

"Atención pasajeros del vuelo 2447 de Panagra con destino al Aeropuerto Iternacional de Miami. Favor de abordar por la Puerta número 7 en el Pasillo Internacional. Por favor tengan sus boletos a la mano para el agente en la puerta de abordaje. Abordarán los pasajeros de primera clase ahora."

"Attention passengers for Panagra Flight 2447, to Miami International Airport. Please board from Gate 7 on the International Concourse. Please have your tickets available for the agent at the gate. We will board our First Class passengers now."

Ted was barely aware of the announcement that had just been made. He was deep in thought. *In our universe, we have no choice but to accept the possibility that bad things will happen to both good* and *bad people because it's simply a basic, fundamental fact of life. Everything in our lives tends toward disorder. It's the price we pay for having life itself.*

"Todos los pasajeros del vuelo 2447 de Panagra con destino al Aeropuerto Internacional de Miami pueden abordar el vuelo ahora. Esta es la última llamada para abordar."

"All passengers for Panagra Flight 2447 with destination Miami International Airport may board now. This is the final boarding call."

By now, Ted was alone in the waiting room.

"Excuse me, señor; do you have a ticket for this flight?"

It was the gate attendant. "We are about to close the gate, señor. If you are on this flight, you better hurry. They are just about to pull the stairs away from the plane."

Ted grabbed his coat, showed the attendant his ticket, and with his gravimeter case and carry-on luggage in hand, ran down the passageway to the stairs leading to the tarmac. He just made it up the stairs and through the cabin door as the stewardess was reaching out to pull the door shut.

"Welcome aboard, señor. Enjoy your flight to Miami."

Those were the best words that Ted had heard in the last four months. They almost sounded like a blessing. The tensions and worries of the last four months slowly melted away as the aircraft gained altitude, climbing high above the clouds and snow-capped Andes to reveal a starlit sky dominated by the Southern Cross.[195] He was at long last on his way home to the warmth of Susan and family.

---

[195] http://www.windows.ucar.edu/the_universe/crux.html

Epilogue

Three years now had passed since Ted returned from Antarctica. He and Susan were married in late January, 1964, between semesters at the University of Wisconsin–Madison, and the only time either of them had free before the end of the school year. They stayed in Madison while Susan completed her Bachelor's degree and Ted continued his studies toward a Doctorate in Geophysics.

Life settled into predictable, easy rhythms. He enthused in the beauty of the Wisconsin springs, summers, and falls, and relaxed in the warmth of his marriage to Susan. The sleepless nights and occasional nightmares that marked the first few months after his return from Antarctica faded with time, though he never could break free from the awful memories of having been trapped in the ice with almost no hope of survival. He thought constantly about his friend, Commander Cristian Barbudo, and what more he could have done to help the man.

Whenever he had the opportunity, Ted pored over the various Chilean newspapers to which the Geophysical and Polar Research Center subscribed, for example, Santiago's *El Mercurio,* to see if there was mention of the theft from the bank in Talcahuano following the Great Chilean Earthquake of 1960. He found nothing.

Nor did anyone he asked in the Department of Geology and Geophysics or at the Center recall hearing or seeing anything unusual related to the return of the 16th Chilean Expedition or to Expedition-related events in the years following the return of the Expeditionary personnel.

He hoped that Captain Muñoz had been true to his word, that he had at the least seen to it that Maria and her two children were taken care of—certainly the Chilean Navy must provide for the families of those who died in its service as well—and that in the end, justice had been served.

Then, early in 1965, a postcard arrived, from Brazil, of all places—a postcard from Maria! Despite the simplicity of the address, the card had made its way to Ted at the Center. The postcard arrived almost three years to the day that he had returned to the United States from Antarctica.

Sugarloaf Mountain (in Portuguese, *Pão de Açúcar*), is a peak situated in Rio de Janeiro, Brazil, at the mouth of Guanabara Bay on a peninsula that juts out into the Atlantic Ocean.[196]

196 See, for example, http://en.wikipedia.org/wiki/Sugarloaf_Mountain_(Brazil)

Pão de Açúcar - Rio de Janeiro, Brazil

O complexo do Pão de Açúcar, localizado no bairro da Urca e composto pelo morro do Pão de Açúcar (que dá nome ao complexo), morro da Urca e morro da Babilônia, é, juntamente com a estátua do Cristo Redentor, o maior cartão postal da cidade do Rio de Janeiro e um dos mais famosos do Brasil.

CORREIO AÉREO

4 marzo 1965
Mí estímado Teodoro,
Roberto y yo le desean un muy próspero Año Nuevo lleno de la salud y la felicidad buenas.
Maria

Sr. Teodoro Stone
Polar Research Center
The Highlands
Madison, Wisconsin,
USA

Maria's message is: "My dear Theodore, Robert and I wish you a very Happy New Year filled with good health and happiness. Maria"

Hmmmmm, thought Ted, *Captain Muñoz appears to be looking after Maria, just as Cristian had asked. But what happened to Roberto's career with the Chilean Navy? Is he still even* in *the Navy? And why is the card mailed from Rio de Janeiro? Are they married? Are they on vacation? Have they left Chile for all time? If they've left the country,* why *did they?*

And what happened to the loot taken from the bank in Talcahuano? What, if any, was Roberto's involvement in the investigation of the theft? Was Roberto behind the whole thing to begin with?

Even if he wasn't, what part, if any, did Roberto play in the murders of Chief Warrant Officer Raul Lucero and Chief Petty Officer Eduardo Bellolio? Should I have withheld the information revealed to me by Cristian from Captain Muñoz and given it instead to the Commodore? These were the two questions that haunted him most. They were his *demons,* and he feared they would be with him the rest of his days.

I guess that in life as in science, Ted tried to reason, *there are questions to which we will* never *know the answers . . . questions for which there are no paradigms, formulae, or guidelines that can be used to illuminate the path to a solution . . . no calculus that when applied, will lead, infinitesimal step by infinitesimal step, to the intrinsic* truth *of the matter.*

In the end, he found cold comfort in his understanding of the events that occurred at the bottom of the world during the austral summer of 1961-1962.

Breinigsville, PA USA
23 November 2010
249949BV00003B/69/P